CHINESE RED

Persons this *Mystery* is about—

QUINNY HITE,
amiable Times Square detective and ex-copper, has his own inimitable way of getting into, and out of, trouble. He is usually at least one brain wave ahead of the police—and is the first to admit it.

CHINESE RED,
a lovely Oriental girl with flame-colored hair, is known to some as Sonya Novatoff. As a glamour girl she stacks up with the best of them, but to Tony Austen, café-society playboy, she was just a novelty—or was she?

QUONG CHEE,
Chinese Red's guardian, is proprietor of Chungking Garden, the most popular restaurant in Chinatown. He is intelligent, but suffers from a horror of enclosed places.

INSPECTOR PIERSON,
Quinny's one-time boss, and one of the best murder men on the force, has one big fault. He's in too much of a hurry to get results.

MAYO BROWNE,
a tall, handsome playboy who attends to the details of Tony Austen's parties, has his future vested, he says, in a couple of goddesses. And because of Tony he may lose them both.

FANE GORDON,
sullen and husky-voiced beauty, is the season's glamour girl. Fane is a brat, but perhaps she is not to be blamed for the fact that she has an aunt who has made a three-ring circus of her.

DEE FORBES,
last year's glamour child, is a pretty blonde whose father got himself on a financial limb bringing her out, and then "fell" from a ten-story window.

RITA CAMONEZ,
a Latin good-looker with plenty of zip, has been making a play for Mayo Browne, but her rich father has a set of steel-rigged requirements to apply to prospective sons-in-law.

PEGGY LONG,
smart and attractive, makes her living by listening more than she talks.

SHERRY GATES,
a tall, slouching Broadway columnist, is inclined to talk a little too much for his own good.

DAVE and WARD KELTON,
about as useless a pair as ever chiseled a drink in 52nd Street, are suffering from the fact that the Kelton bankroll died off before the family did.

CHINESE RED

What this *Mystery* is about—

● ● ● A WRINKLED SUIT that upsets a wedding . . . A sacred JAPANESE KNIFE that must draw blood whenever it is unsheathed . . . THE BODY of a rich playboy strangely crumpled in a phony opium den . . . A trail of SPOTS, near the scene of a murder, that are visible only in the dark . . . A bloodstained white EVENING JACKET . . . A man's GOLD BRACELET that is said to conceal $10,000 in pocket money . . . Two RUBBER CHECKS, canceled but not paid, that keep on bouncing around . . . A weirdly glowing STATUE of a Chinese moon goddess that holds a strong fascination for a number of people . . . A DOOR painted red for luck . . . A PLUCKED CHICKEN that goes on a strange journey . . . A grim RIDE taken by a detective and a Chinese girl with red hair . . . A scarlet CARNATION.

Wouldn't You Like to Know—

- How Quinny Hite becomes an involuntary hero and thereby meets· murder?
- Why the wealthy playboy and his friends went on a junket to Chinatown?
- How the body got into the opium den?
- Whose stealthy hand reached into the raincoat pocket?
- Why Quinny has a suspect arrested just so he can have him sprung?

YOU will learn the answers to these questions in this chuckle-packed mystery in which Quinny Hite is caught out of his usual Times Square orbit—between the strange worlds of café society and New York's Chinatown.

A *QUINNY HITE* MURDER MYSTERY

CHINESE RED

By RICHARD BURKE

Author of "Here Lies the Body,"
"The Dead Take No Bows,"
"The Frightened Pigeon," etc.

Author's Dedication—
For NANCY and W. S.

WILDSIDE PRESS

CHINESE RED

List of *Exciting* Chapters—

Chinese Red

Chapter One

OVERBOARD!

IT WAS A LITTLE WHITE CHURCH with a solid-looking steeple, like the smaller ones to be seen on wedding cakes. This one was real, however, nestled in the trees at the side of a lane near New Dorp. On a bright, sunny day it would have been charming in its rural setting, but the country loses a good bit of its attraction in wet weather. This was a rainy day.

On the broad steps, sheltered somewhat from the drizzle, stood a group of people: a minister, a girl in bridal array, two other girls, and an older woman, all staring anxiously up the lane toward its intersection with the main highway—Amboy Road. Another man sat at the opposite end of the steps, resting his elbows on his knees, his gaze fixed on nothing at all of which he was conscious. Quinny Hite, this was, private detective and prospective bridegroom, at last brought to the altar by Joan Fairley. Strictly speaking, she'd only got him to the church steps. Quinny wasn't offering any resistance, but a serious hitch had developed: Johnny Littlebird.

This church-wedding idea had been entirely Joan's. In the detective's circle, people seldom were married anywhere but at the chapel in the Municipal Building —if at all. Joan, however, after two failures to take legal possession of her man at the Park Row marriage counter, and having had both tries nullified by circumstances either unforeseen or uncontrollable, had enlarged her plans. Now it had to be a church affair, with a couple of bridesmaids and her aunt as matron of honor, down in the remote fastnesses of Staten Island. She had also exceeded a bride's privileges by choosing the best man, picking Johnny Littlebird for the office, a selection based on his decorative value and knowledge of correct social form.

Quinny, while not caring very much who attended him, hadn't the same feeling about Johnny. In his considered opinion, the man was a first-rate heel. Sure, Johnny knew all about etiquette, but he never used any. Circumstances now tended to prove this. It was long past the appointed hour for the ceremony. Someone had been whanging away on an organ inside the church for an hour, and Quinny was getting pretty well bored with nuptial music. Johnny Littlebird had not shown up.

The nonappearance of the best man at a wedding may not ordinarily be complete disaster, but this time it was. Joan, distrusting Quinny to do anything right, had given the marriage license to Johnny along with the commission to deliver the groom at the altar at 3:00 p.m. After a bachelor breakfast in the Automat at high noon, the pair were to descend on New Dorp by subway, ferry, and bus and meet the rest of the party at the church, bringing flowers. Specifically, flowers of Johnny's selection. Joan wouldn't put it past Quinny to show up with a floral gates-ajar if that happened to be all that was left over at the undertaking place on Eighth Avenue.

For a good two hours Quinny had waited for his best man, breakfasting meanwhile on a pair of doughnuts, a piece of apple pie, and three or four cups of coffee. As two o'clock came around and Johnny Littlebird did not, he decided to set off for Staten Island on his own. He was mildly surprised at Johnny, since he had agreed to pay him five dollars plus transportation for his services. Anyhow, he was in five bucks, and one doesn't actually need a best man to get married. He went into the Astor Flower Shop and paid, to him, an appalling sum for a mess of posies for Joan, then started for Staten Island. The matter of Johnny's possession of the marriage license didn't occur to him until it was pointed out on the steps of the church in New Dorp.

In justice to Johnny Littlebird, the nonappearance wasn't his idea at all but the result of mental carelessness. A sartorial fancy Dan, Johnny would no more appear at a wedding in a suit even slightly out of press than he would with bare feet and spats. The suit he had elected to wear seemed in something less than perfect condition, so he stopped in Moe the Tailor's shop to have it pressed. He disrobed behind the sleazy curtain of the cubicle designed for one-suit guys in need of pressing and passed out the garment. He should have remembered that there was a balance due on this self-same suit, a matter of three dollars. Moe the Tailor, an opportunist with Times Square training, foreclosed the mortgage on the suit at once.

It was stalemate. Moe had the clothes, Johnny did not have three dollars. Moe didn't seem to care much about Johnny's social engagements, even though the latter pointed out that, with the five-dollar fee he was to receive as best man, he could lift the lien on the suit. Moe also expressed indifference as to what Johnny wore to return to his room, or whether he wore anything. On the other hand, the tailor wasn't especially attracted to the idea of having Johnny occupy the dressing cubicle indefinitely. A substitute idea came to him. His colored man was off for the day with a misery in his stomach. Moe suggested that Johnny could literally iron out his difficulties by pressing suits at fifty cents an hour until the three-dollar debt was cleared up. The ensuing argument was bitter, profane, but short. Moe, having much the better strategic position, won, and Johnny moved into the back room to begin his work for freedom. At fifty cents an hour, freedom would be attained about dark. Meanwhile, the wedding party was stalled on the steps of the little white church in New Dorp.

"If you ask me, this wedding is just another flop!" exclaimed one of the bridesmaids, named Ninon Natchette (which Quinny seemed to think was a post-christening selection).

"Did anybody ask?" growled Quinny. "*I* didn't."

"Johnny wouldn't do a thing like this to me," asserted Joan, her eyes unhappy, but showing signs of growing temper.

Quinny lifted a hand and waved it limply. "Use your own judgment, babe," he said. "So far, it ain't been good, but go on using it. We're here. Johnny isn't—"

The other bridesmaid spoke. "And it wouldn't surprise me a bit if you knew *why* he isn't!"

"Maybe I do," returned the detective, resuming his inspection of the trees across the lane. "On form, I'd say Johnny met a dame. He's weak, that way—nothing he wouldn't do for a good-looking, warm-eyed gal. One he ain't seen before, that is."

"Not like you," said the bride with heavy sarcasm.

"Not like me," affirmed Quinny. "I don't do anything for dames. They do things for me. Such as pickin' out a heel like Johnny to be my best man—"

"I don't think it's Johnny's fault," interrupted Joan hotly. "You didn't go to the right Automat, or something."

Quinny pulled the smart new derby down a little firmer and relapsed into silence. He couldn't win—and he knew it. At five the minister regretfully announced that he wouldn't be able to wait any longer, as he was due at the parsonage for tea. The organ player had already left.

"Tea?" Quinny hoisted an eyebrow and stared earnestly at the minister. "You mean—*tea?*"

"We might as well go home, Joan," the girl's aunt said. She added cheerily, "Better luck next time, I always say!"

Joan shook her head. "This is three strikes," she said. "Quinny and I just aren't meant to be married. It's Fate—that's what it is. Fate!"

"It's Johnny Littlebird—" Quinny began.

"I'm through!" continued the girl, dabbing at her eyes with a bit of linen. "This is the finish, Quinny. Tomorrow I'm going to take that San Francisco job Murray's been wanting me for. I've got to forget you."

"Aw, now, Jones—" In his softer moods, the detective invariably substituted "Jones" for "Joan."

"We—we'll always be friends." Joan took a tentative step down. "Come on, Auntie—take me home."

Quinny stared at her with a frustrated expression. He had never felt any deep enthusiasm about this getting married business, but all of a sudden, with his prospective bride walking out on him, he realized that he was really quite keen about becoming her husband.

"You'll feel different tomorrow," he said hopefully.

"No. Never." Joan held out a slim white hand that shook a little. "Good-by now."

Quinny took the soft hand in his. He didn't know what to say in a situation like this. No girl had ever given him the brush-off before, he thought. He just didn't remember. Eyes swimming with tears, Joan walked away on the arm of her aunt, the detective looking after them, bewildered. He did tip his derby, though.

Quinny set off on the return trip to Manhattan, with a pair of near-bridesmaids in escort. There hadn't been any way of avoiding it. These two night-club hands didn't intend to let an opportunity like this slip away. They had a number of insults in mind to add to the injury already sustained by the detective.

"You know, Ninon, I gave a fella the air like this once," said one. She shifted her blue but not baby eyes to Quinny and went on suggestively, "He shot himself."

Quinny returned her gaze coldly. "At that, he was lucky," he commented.

"Now that the wedding is off," Ninon cut in, "I suppose you'll find yourself a corpse to find the murderer of. Just to make it a day."

"With a nice fat fee for some bookie to take away from you," supplemented the other. "What a dope you are, Quinny Hite!"

"If the corpse was Johnny Littlebird, I'd crack the case for free," returned Quinny, morosely. "Just to shake hands with the mug that done it."

Once aboard the big ferryboat which plies between Staten Island and lower Manhattan, Quinny shook off the girls, taking refuge on the lower deck, up near the bow (if a ferryboat really has a bow). He sat down on the running-board of a car to consider what he would do with the rest of the day. The first thing, he decided, was to look up the errant best man as soon as he got back to Times Square, not to demand an accounting, but to bop him one on the jaw. This gesture would be necessary to restore, in a measure, Quinny's peace of mind. He glanced ahead toward the mist-shrouded skyline of Manhattan, as though measuring the distance still to be traversed. For comfort he had removed his coat and had it carefully folded across his lap.

The ferryboat thumped solidly along and then, abruptly, the detective was roused from his brooding by the sound of shouts coming from the deck overhead. The few passengers near him were rushing to the rail, and someone yelled, "Man overboard!"

Quinny leaped up and started on a dash for the rail to see what was going on, his coat remaining where he'd let it slide out of his lap. He headed for the open section at the end of the boat, the apron, not noticing that it was wet with spray and rain, and the instant he reached it his feet shot out from under him as though the deck were greased. Unluckily he didn't stop there, but continued as though sliding for second base. He skidded right on past the end of the rail, zoomed out briefly in mid-air, and came down in a spectacular though unorthodox dive into the choppy water of the bay.

Like most New Yorkers raised in the vicinity of the West Side docks, Quinny was a capable swimmer. Regaining the surface, he saw that the ferryboat was now some distance away, back-pedaling vigorously with its propellers. Another quick glance revealed the low shore of Governor's Island about, so to speak, three points on his starboard bow. Having little respect for the skill of ferryboat crews in small boat work, he started off for the island, handicapped by his remaining clothes and still not wanting to shed them. It was a brand-new suit.

He hadn't taken more than a half-dozen strokes when something soft bumped into him and he felt a firm grip on one of his ankles. Looking back over his shoulder, he discovered a soggy, waterlogged person clinging to his foot—probably the man who had gone overboard first.

"Leggo!" said Quinny firmly.

The command was disregarded, and the detective was about to kick out vigorously to break the hold when the man was rolled over on his back by the violent waves of the ferryboat's wake. The face exposed was one of agonized terror, the unreasoning panic of a person about to drown. Quinny realized this episode had a very good chance of terminating in the drowning of both. He twisted around, doubling himself up to bring the stranger closer, and lashed out furiously with his fist at the other man's jaw. The man relaxed his hold, rolled helplessly a moment in the seaway, then began to sink.

Quinny grabbed him by the back of his coat and hauled him back to the surface. *You can't just let a man drown,* he thought, and, as a wave lifted them, he looked to see if anyone else was doing anything about it. The ferryboat had come to a stop, and he saw men struggling with a lifeboat on the upper deck. *They'll take till dark, those mugs,* he thought, shaking the water from his eyes. Then he saw the tugboat and felt better about the situation. This was a cocky little craft with *Winnifred* in block letters on the wheelhouse and it was rushing through the water toward him.

Meanwhile, what might have been other assistance, but was now a decided menace, was approaching from the other direction. This was a huge balk of wood, drifting aimlessly about the lower harbor, a hazard to any small craft that might encounter it—and also a hazard to Quinny. His eyes were now intent on the approaching tug, and as it drew near he wondered what the lug in the bow was yelling and gesticulating about.

Rising and falling each time a wave passed under it, one end of the big timber would lift momentarily, then drop heavily into the water. In another minute it was going to come down on the struggling detective. The shouting deckhand was defeating his own purpose by keeping Quinny's attention on the tug. Otherwise the detective might have heard the squash of the timber dropping into the trough.

Propellers churning in reverse, the tug slid through the water. The deckhand reached out with a long boat-hook, which Quinny twisted into the helpless man's coat and then let go.

"Watch out!" screamed the deckhand, pointing at the floating beam with one hand and pulling in on the boathook with the other.

Quinny started to turn his head to see what the deckhand was pointing at, but it was too late. The world seemed to crash about him, something roared in his ears, and flashing lights bewildered his brain. He sighed, relaxed, and began sinking into a wet, silent space.

Chapter Two

CHUNGKING GARDEN

THE SCENT OF FLOWERS filled the air, and he seemed to be lying on his back with hands folded across his chest. As consciousness slowly filtered into the jarred cranium, Quinny pondered the question of whether he was still alive, or dead in his coffin. If this was a coffin he was stretched out in, it was much more comfortable than his bed at the Hotel du Nord. Also, he felt as if he were enclosed in silken garments, a new experience and for that reason creating fresh doubt of his still being alive.

Quinny could faintly hear an orchestra, which was all right, except that "Chattanooga Choo-Choo" wasn't his idea of a dirge. Maybe they were burying him to swing music, just to be different. He listened carefully for a few moments. If it *was* a funeral—*his* funeral—somebody ought to be crying. He didn't know just who, except Joan, but she was mad at him. Joan had once said something about his not even showing up for his own funeral. Now it seemed a fair bet he'd not only shown up, but ahead of time.

Soft footsteps sounded in the gloom just as he discovered that he could use his hands—there didn't really seem to be anything wrong with them now that he'd made the try. He started to raise them in a move to stop anyone from screwing down the lid of the casket, if that was what they were up to, when a click sounded and a light came on.

Much to his bewilderment, Quinny found himself well enveloped in a commodious bed. It was quite a bed, with carved dragons forming its four posts, and the spread like nothing the detective had seen before. His eyes encountered the placid gaze of a Chinese girl, dressed in a black outfit that looked like pajamas.

Quinny tried a grin. His head was clearing up rapidly now, even if the situation wasn't.

"Hello," he said. "Glad you came in. I was just wondering whether I was dead or not. Seems I ain't."

The girl stood there, not moving a muscle of her oval-shaped face while he was speaking, then turned her head and spoke rapidly in Chinese as though to someone in the next room. Turning to the detective again, she said, "No speak ingriss."

Another person, a small, middle-aged Chinese, entered the room. He came to the bedside and stood looking down at Quinny with a broad smile on his pleasant face. The girl, with a glance at the newcomer, went out.

"You are feeling better?" the stranger asked, almost without accent.

"I feel okay," replied Quinny. "But how did I make the jump from New York harbor to here?"

"You do not remember," said the Chinese, nodding his head. "You do not remember jumping from the ship to help a man who had just been stupid enough to fall overboard?"

Quinny quite clearly remembered, but his version was slightly different. He had fallen overboard himself, without planning to rescue anyone. For the moment, though, he decided not to stress this difference.

"Yes, I remember that," he agreed. "And just as me

and the other mug were about to be picked up, something socked me. You fill in from there."

"I am Quong Chee—the man you tried to, and did, help," said the Chinese. "I am more grateful than I have words to express. But for your action I should now be at the bottom of the bay. I myself have no recollection of what happened until I recovered on the towing-boat, but I was told that as we were about to be taken from the water a large piece of driftwood struck you on the head. You were saved from destruction, fortunately, by the derby hat you wore, which softened the blow."

"I bet the kelly's a wreck," mourned Quinny. "It was a new one, too."

"I have preserved the hat," resumed the Chinese. "With the thought that you might like to keep it. You see, when I had fully recovered, there was the question of what to do with you. There was nothing in your clothes—you had lost your coat—with which you could be identified. When the boat reached an East River pier, I had you brought here—to my home—with me. Your injury is slight, but my debt to you is great."

Let it be like that, thought the detective, dismissing any idea of relating the facts of his plunge into the water.

"If you will tell me where to send, I will have someone bring you other clothes. Those you had on are still wet and, without the coat, incomplete."

Quinny pursed his lips. This wasn't much of a problem. His only other suit was hanging where he'd left it in the closet of his room at the du Nord. It wasn't much of a suit, either, but it would have to do. He gave the information to Quong Chee, adding that he had better call the hotel to make sure the suit would be turned over to the messenger.

"Yes," said Quong Chee, nodding again. "Meanwhile, your dinner will be served here."

With a fond look and saying he would return presently, Quong Chee left the room, and the detective relaxed to survey the situation. There was little to survey. When he had dined and got into dry clothes, he would go back uptown. Within a couple of hours he thought he could locate Johnny Littlebird, the author of the day's trials, and settle things with him. Johnny usually spent the greater part of the evening in Shubert Alley, a fine hunting-ground for one of his masculine charm. Through this alley pass the most beautiful showgirls in New York. Quinny had it in mind to make Shubert Alley a hunting-ground of a different sort, with Johnny the quarry.

The Chinese girl returned, this time with a small tray bearing a glass of white liqueur, which she put down on a bedside table. The detective picked up the glass and smelled it curiously. It had the odor of rose petals. He glanced up at the girl, with a questioning lift of his eyebrows.

"*Mu kwai lu,*" said the girl.

Double talk, eh? thought Quinny. "Me cwy you, too," he answered, wiggling his eyebrows.

"Man drink," said the girl, unmoved. "*Mu kwai lu.*"

He got it now. This last crack was in Chinese, he decided. His Chinese vocabulary was limited to *ho la ma,* and he wasn't even sure what this phrase meant.

"Something to drink, eh?" he said, sniffing at the contents of the glass. "Smells like shave lotion. Okay—here goes."

He tossed it off, finding it smooth if sweetish, but it produced a glow in his stomach that hadn't been there before. He leaned back against the pillows, tolerably content with this world where he found himself. If only the girl could speak English, or he could speak Chinese! She was a darned good-looker, and there was something odd about her that he found attractive. Her figure was slender and well formed, her hands long and shapely, with bright red nail polish. He couldn't give her much on hair-do, though. It was severe, with a fringe of bangs straight across her forehead, in the Chinese manner, but somehow it didn't seem to him quite right.

A waiter brought enough dinner to feed him and a number of his friends, had they been lucky enough to be present. Then the girl disappeared, leaving him to a full if lonely enjoyment of the viands. He spent some time at it, with pauses to admire the resplendent pajamas in which he was encased.

Quinny had never seen a room like this, either, nor have many people without Chinese friends to visit. It was furnished in the austere manner which upper-class Chinese seem to like. Beside the bed was a black teakwood stand on which was a large bowl of narcissus blooms. A single straight-backed chair stood against one wall under a Chinese print. That was all.

Must be the guest room, soliloquized the detective. *They fixed it up like this so's their guests won't move in for keeps.*

Sometime later Quong Chee reappeared, trailed by a Chinese boy carrying a badly wrapped package. Quinny's old brown suit. Not much to start with, it had suffered in transit. Quong Chee sent it downstairs to a tailorshop for pressing.

"What's going on out there?" inquired Quinny, lolling back against the luxurious pillows. "Every time somebody comes in or goes out I hear music."

The Chinese explained that the apartment adjoined Chungking Garden, a restaurant of which he took some small pride in being the proprietor. The detective knew the restaurant very well by reputation. It was one of the largest and best in Chinatown, a district of countless eating-houses. Chungking Garden was definitely considered the place to go when doing Chinatown, or even if the visitor merely wanted Chinese food sufficiently to come downtown after it. Situated on the top floor of an old building, it had been transformed by skillful decorators into a striking interpretation of a Chinese interior.

It was nearing nine o'clock when the detective finally got himself assembled in the old brown suit, which didn't somehow look the same with the wrinkles removed. He donned the new derby his host had obtained for him from a Chatham Square haberdasher and surveyed himself in a full-length mirror set in the bathroom door. He looked pretty good, he decided. There was going to be a new suit, too, Quong Chee had promised him, as soon as Quinny could get around to having one fitted. The way the old brown one looked, though, he needn't be in a hurry, unless Joan relented and decided to have another go at getting married.

Quinny sauntered out of the apartment, which opened onto one end of a long mezzanine balcony extending around two sides of the restaurant underneath. He paused for a moment at the railing to look down at the dining-room. The bad weather seemed to have had a depressing effect on business—there were not many diners present in the main room, and none at all on the mezzanine. Two or three couples were dancing on the small dance floor to the music he had heard back in the apartment. Seeing a flight of stairs up ahead of him which led down to the side of the dance space, he walked slowly in that direction between the dimly lighted tables.

At the head of the stairway he found a Chinese girl, standing with her back toward him as he approached. At first he didn't know she was Chinese. Quinny could see only a pile of flaming red hair above the high-collared sequin jacket, and gray jade pendants hanging from her ears. When she turned her head, he was surprised to find that this gorgeous creature was just as Chinese as the girl who'd brought him the unpronounceable drink in the apartment. In fact, she looked like the same one—but that one had black hair, as Chinese are supposed to have.

"Hello," Quinny greeted her. "Waitin' for me?"

"Well, no," replied the girl, smiling faintly. "Did you enjoy your dinner? I hope you did."

"You should know," he said. He suddenly knew that this *was* the same girl he'd seen before, plus a red wig. "What's the idea of pulling that 'no speak' stuff on me? Also, how come the red wig? Didn't you know Chinese don't have red hair?"

The girl tugged vigorously at a wisp of hair. "But this is not a wig!" she said. "It is my own hair."

"You wasn't a redhead the last time I saw you," accused Quinny, skeptically.

"Yes, I was," she said, with a small, rippling laugh.

"The black hair you saw was a wig I ordinarily wear, because my own hair is so conspicuous where everyone's hair is black."

Quinny nodded. "And right now you want to get noticed," he said. "Any special reason? I mean about showing off now?" He looked her over appraisingly. "You'd stand out anytime, anywhere, with hair like that!"

"This is my moment to be conspicuous," she replied, with a graceful motion of her hand to indicate the dance floor below. "I am one of the presumed attractions of Chungking Garden. I am about to open the floor show, just as soon as the dancing is finished."

"What do you do?" asked the detective. "Sing? Dance? Don't tell me you're a stripper. If you are, I'll stay around and catch your act."

"No. I do little except to open the show in my naïve Chinese manner," she explained, her eyes shining with amusement at Quinny's disappointed expression. "And then, at the end, to close it."

"Just a talking act, eh?" he commented, losing some of his interest. "Where'll I find your old man? Like to tell him good night and thanks for everything."

"My father is buried in Leningrad," she said. "You might like to know that he was a Russian—therefore my red hair. But, if it is Quong Chee you wish to see, you may find him in his office at the other end of this balcony."

"Okay, thanks. Say, what's your name? You know, in case I wanted to call you up sometime."

She chuckled. "They call me Chinese Red," she answered.

Quinny stared at her for a moment. "I like you!" he

said, abruptly.

The girl laughed again and turned toward the stairway. "Me cwy you, too," she said.

"Oh, yeah," replied Quinny. "That reminds me; you didn't tell me yet why you pulled the 'no speak' stuff on me a while ago."

"Mellican man maybe flesh guy. Better no spik."

"Um!" grunted the detective, understandingly.

The restaurant lights began to dim, and Chinese Red moved down the stairs. The show was about to begin. Quinny leaned on the mezzanine railing to watch for a minute or two before going on to Quong Chee's office. A spotlight picked up the descending figure of the girl as she proceeded down the broad staircase, the railings of which were the tails of two huge dragons curving down to the heads with widely opened, upturned mouths forming newel posts at the bottom. The orchestra had begun the soft strains of the entrance music from *Chu Chin Chow,* gradually swelling as the girl swayed gracefully from step to step. She ignored the small audience entirely until she had reached the dance floor. Then she began announcing the show to follow.

Someone applauded noisily before she finished, and Quinny glanced around to see who it was, locating the offender in a booth in the far corner. A party seemed to be in progress there, three women in evening clothes sitting at a table set for eight.

Not at all interested in the show, Quinny walked on around the mezzanine to Quong's offices. There was an outer office, with two windows overlooking the restaurant floor, and an inner office with just one window which opened onto a four-foot-wide strip of roof between the mezzanine floor (which had been added to

the building later) and the street wall of the building.
No view of the dining-room was to be had from this
inner office. An enclosed, narrow stairway led from it to
the checkroom in the foyer below, serving Quong Chee
as a sometimes more convenient way to his office from
the elevator. The door to these stairs was closed, and the
detective supposed it was a closet.

The Chinese wasn't in either of his offices, nor anyone else, so Quinny came out again. He started back to
the stairway which led to the main floor, but stopped
to sit at a table and look at the show. It was now in full
blast—a noisy comedy act by three white men holding
the floor. Two girls—a sister team—had just finished
their turn, without bows. The shadowy figure of a man
in dark trousers and white coat passed behind Quinny
and went on toward the offices, but the detective saw
him just as he was disappearing through the door. He
got up and followed, thinking it was Quong Chee, who
had been wearing a white coat, but found no one in the
outer office. Hearing a sound from the other room, he
crossed to look in. He was mildly surprised to find no
one there, either. He didn't bother further with finding
Quong Chee.

"Damned clever, these Chinese," he grunted, unorigi-
nally, and, returning to the stairs, descended to the
main floor, crossing to the foyer he saw on the other
side.

He found, to his gratification, that Chungking Garden was serviced by a small elevator, operated by a
youthful Chinese who, on nights when business was
dull, also attended the checkroom which adjoined the
foyer.

"Check coat, run erevator—all the time wuk, wuk,

wuk!" complained the boy as he took Quinny down.

"What are you kicking about?" asked the detective. "You only have four floors in the joint."

"Th'ee," corrected the boy. "Th'ee flo'. Cerrar, number one flo', top flo'. No two, no th'ee flo'."

Quinny figured this out as meaning the car served only the basement, ground floor, and restaurant. Later he found that the second and third floors were cut up into a maze of small rooms occupied by countless Chinese who used the cubicles for both living and business purposes. These rooms were reached by means of the main stairway of the building. When the elevator was installed, however, exits to all the floors had been provided and were still usable. It is doubtful that the Chinese would have bothered to use the elevator even if service had been supplied.

The detective fished a cigarette from a package in his coat pocket and then made an unsuccessful exploration for a match. The elevator boy handed him a packet, and Quinny applied the flame of one to the cigarette. His brows came together in a scowl as he saw a moist red spot on the back of his hand. It looked like blood. He got out a handkerchief and wiped it off, inspecting the skin for some sort of trifling injury to account for the blood. There wasn't even a scratch. Mildly curious about the blood spot, he left the car when it reached the main floor and headed for the street.

The building lobby was quite deserted as he walked through toward the front doors, where he stopped for a moment to stare disapprovingly at the wet street, with the reflection that Chungking Garden most likely was in for a quiet night.

He'd never entertained a more erroneous thought.

Chapter Three

THE MAN WHO WOULDN'T WAKE UP

PRACTICALLY EVERYONE in these days knows what China-town looks like, be it New York, San Francisco, or the settlements of smaller cities, but what goes on behind the façades of these districts is less obvious. The casual sightseer sees much that is strange to him and by liberal use of his imagination is inclined to make things appear even stranger. This all comes out even, however, as the Chinese undoubtedly regard the tourist as being a pretty queer form of human life also. Chinatown for the Chinese comes into its own in the hours after midnight, when the visitors from uptown and points north, south, and west have returned to the fancied security of their own civilization. The sensations of the dwellers in these shabby buildings must be akin to those of their white brother when the week-end guest goes home.

Doyers Street, shortest of the three main thoroughfares of New York's Chinatown, is also the most Chinese. Not really much more than an L-shaped alley, the old buildings facing on it probably house more human beings per square foot than any tenement in the metropolis.

Light rain was still falling as Quinny emerged from Chungking Garden onto the sidewalk, and traffic was at a minimum. Just a few Chinese scurrying along under large umbrellas, and one or two white men who evidently had wandered in from the neighboring flophouse district of the Bowery. The detective took shelter before the window of a small periodical shop next to the building entrance, where he eyed the display with passive interest.

Rain dripped down the back of his coat collar from the fire escape overhead, and he lost interest in Oriental literature, scuttling along toward an awning over the front of a Chinese grocery in the same building. He didn't reach it. Steps from the basement were between the magazine shop and grocery, and as he slithered along he collided with a bulky person just emerging. The stranger cursed—in English—but broke off as he recognized the detective and was recognized in return.

Honey Joe Hix was an old acquaintance of the detective, dating from the days when both had attended P. S. 3, down on Hudson and Grove Streets. Since then Quinny had matriculated into the police force, risen by uneasy stages to the rank of detective, first class, and subsequently been bounced for alleged irregularities in the disposal of forbidden news tips to his favorite newspaper. Hix, meanwhile, had wandered off into the hinterland with various carnivals and medicine shows, graduating therefrom with honors as a grade-A pitchman, grifter, and promoter—of a sort. The name Honey Joe stemmed from his constant use of the word "honey" to describe anything of which he approved.

"Well, well!" exclaimed Honey Joe exuberantly. "If it ain't old Homicide Hite himself! If you're down here looking for a dragon—there ain't any. What used to be the dragon is a lion now."

Quinny disclaimed interest in either dragons or lions. "What are you doing this far out of Times Square?" he demanded.

"Why—I got a business here," explained Honey Joe.

"A nice clean business like I always wanted to get into. I'm running a hop joint."

"Nice and clean!" commented the detective.

"Yeh-yeh, that's what it is—and it's a honey, I tell you," continued Hix. "Right here in this basement. Of course, there ain't any dope in the joint—ain't been any for twenty or thirty years, I guess. They tell me it used to be a *bony fidie* joint in the old days—you can still smell the stuff."

"I don't want to," objected Quinny, firmly. "Everything smells funny down here."

"Yeh-yeh." Honey Joe was not one to relinquish the lead in a conversation, or even to have it sidetracked. "Maybe it does—like you say—but you don't notice it after a while. The Chinatown bus suckers think it is still a dive and that is okay by me, on account of they pay 25¢ a head to view the horrors of an opium den. Good moral lesson for 'em, and a respectable business for me. I like it—nothin' up the sleeve, everything on the strict up and up. It's a honey, pal, it's a honey—open from noon to midnight. Later, in the busy season."

"You mean there's a regular season for this racket?"

"Sure. You don't think folks are coming down here in hot weather, do you?"

"No!" said the detective decisively. "I don't think even mugs off a rubberneck wagon would want to go prowlin' a stinky basement."

"Aw—wait a minute!" objected Hix, with an injured expression on his florid face. "It don't smell that bad. Not good, maybe—but not so awful as all that. Come on down and have a look."

"Or a sniff."

Quinny followed his friend down the poorly lighted steps to the basement, where, after they had traversed a gloom-shrouded hall with several turns in it, they brought up in the outer room of the ersatz joint, which was about the size of a large closet. There was a window set in the wall separating this room from·one adjoining. Through this opening the detective could see a venerable Chinese apparently doing a bit of bookkeeping with the aid of an abacus. He took time out to examine Quinny with calm and frank curiosity. In actual operation, at this point Hix would collect a quarter from each of the shuddering tourists, hand the lump sum to the Chinese, and escort his covey into the next room. Quinny, of course, was deadheading.

"You know, Quinny, a Chinaman is the only guy I can trust with the dough, if I figure on getting all of it back," explained the entrepreneur sadly. "Chinese are honest."

They entered the room beyond the celestial cashier. This was a forbidding place, with a double tier of wooden bunks lining the walls, the only other furniture being a plain kitchen table and one chair.

"This is the men's smoking lounge," said Hix, with a sweeping gesture of his big hand. "In them there bunks you will see the dregs of the under—"

"Before you go any further, remember I ain't payin'," interrupted the detective, looking curiously at a small brass spirit lamp of Chinese workmanship. The lamp was not lighted at the moment. There were also a couple of cans on the table, partially filled with brown, sticky-looking grease. Quinny picked one up, lifting it to his nose for a tentative sniff at its contents.

"That's phony opium," chuckled Hix. "Them Chinese letters on the label mean *first class ginger.*"

The room reeked with the fumes of cheap sandal-wood incense—frequently mistaken by the sightseers for the odor of opium. They usually held their breath at this point—just in case.

"You was saying something about dregs," prompted the detective. "What dregs?"

"I get bums from Bowery flophouses to stooge as opium smokers," elucidated Hix. "I pay 'em two bits a night, which is good dough for not doin' nothin' harder than layin' on your back lookin' dopey. These mugs look dopey, anyhow, even standin' up, so that's no trouble to 'em."

Hix paused to assume a benevolent expression, and then continued: "Two or three of these bums—if there's that many with a shave—I dress up in tuxes. You know, like you see in *Esquire.* That's to give the place class. These *Esquire* mugs cost me thirty-five cents—"

"What's the extra dime for?"

"Well, they got to be kinda genteel-lookin' and not so damned dirty as the others generally are. That kind of tramps are scarce. They change duds over in a little room back of the Joss House—and say, when them guys get all dolled up, do you think they'll have any-thing to do with the others? No, they will not. Gawd, the airs they put on!

"I also feed all of 'em with leftovers from the restau-rant upstairs—the customers up there never eat more'n half what they order—and where can a Bowery bum do better? Costs me a dime a plate. That's where these zombies are now—scoffin' in the Ladies' Smokin' Par-lor, the next room."

This Ladies' Parlor was a leftover, too, from the days when the place had been a real dive. To keep up the illusion of authenticity, Hix usually had a couple of what he called Sidewalk Annies reposing there in evening gowns at fifty cents a night.

"These Sidewalk Annies are the hardest of all to get," he explained bitterly. "You'd think these dames would jump at a chance to get off the feet for a while, but they don't. Another thing, I gotta watch 'em like a hawk, or they'll sneak out on me with the costumes."

A mere peek into the Ladies' Parlor was more than sufficient for the detective. He turned back into the men's room, ready to leave the whole place, when he noticed a shabby creature lying in one of the bunks at the farther wall.

"What's the matter with that guy over there?" he asked. "Or did he eat already?"

"Well, what d'you know!" exclaimed his host, looking toward the bunk. "A bum passin' up his grub!"

Quinny sauntered over and eyed the derelict with disfavor, but there seemed something odd in the position the man had assumed. It was not the relaxed posture of natural sleep.

"Maybe this guy don't want to eat any more," observed the detective as Hix came to join him.

"Come on, come on, lug! Snap out of that and go get your chow—" shouted Hix, pushing his fist against the man's shoulder. The sleeper made no response. "Hey—the guy's passed out on me! I'm bettin' he's snuck in a flask of alky—the louse! I don't allow drinkin' on the premises, neither—exceptin' by me, of course. Nice reputation this joint'll get, with bums layin' around stinkin' drunk! Hey—alley-oop—" He prodded the unresisting figure once more.

"Wait a minute, Joe," Quinny said. He leaned over the prostrate figure, frowning. "This guy ain't drunk."

"The hell he ain't—" began Hix, stormily.

"He's dead."

The divekeeper recoiled. His lips moved as though to complete what he had been saying, but no sound issued. Then he swallowed with an effort and regained his speech.

"You're—you're kiddin', Quinny!" he exclaimed. "How *can* he be dead? Why, this'll put me out of business! Of all the rotten luck—why does this bum have to pick *my* place to check out in?"

Quinny straightened up, his gaze still on the quiet figure in the bunk. The man was lying partially on his side, his back supported by the board which formed the outer edge of the bunk, and his face was turned toward the wall, the wide-open eyes staring fixedly at— nothing. The collar of the ragged coat was pulled up over the back of his neck, his outstretched hands on the bare boards between the body and the wall.

"This fella's no bum," asserted the detective. "He didn't get that haircut on the Bowery for two bits, and his hands are practically fresh from a manicure. You'll notice by that mark around his left wrist he's been wearing a wrist watch—and lately. This is no bum."

"That makes it all the worse," groaned Hix. "Jees, his face is dirty enough!"

"Yeah. Somebody's smudged it over with some kind of greasy dirt. But the hands are clean."

Quinny pulled back the ragged coat, uncovering a soiled, unbuttoned shirt, which he drew away from the dead man's torso. An ugly, dark red smear came into view—just over the heart. Hix caught his breath sharply.

"He's not only dead—but murdered!" said Quinny. "Notice that he was stabbed, Hix, before these rags were put on him. There's no blood on either the shirt or coat. Also, he's barefooted."

"I'll take your word for it." Hix retreated to the center of the room and stood looking back toward the bunk. "I seen enough. What are you going to do?"

"He looks Park Avenue to me. Kinda familiar, too— like somebody I've seen before." The detective struck a match for closer inspection of the smeared face, then drew back, recognition dawning in his eyes. "You know who this is, Hix? It's that playboy you see pictures of in the tabs all the time, sittin' around in the top-hat nighteries with the latest glamour dames. Tony Austen!"

Chapter Four

GREASE

TONY AUSTEN, whose body reclined in the wooden bunk, had been a good-looking six-footer in his early thirties, a wealthy young man who had added greatly to a backlog of inherited wealth through shrewd and aggressive business methods. He had liked making money for the feeling of superiority it brought, and lavished large sums in the Fifty-second Street night spots for much the same reason. Here he spent most of his leisure hours, feeding his ego on the adulation of his own section of café society. Quite too many of his night-club pals made a business of providing ego food.

"Funny place for a man like Tony Austen to get knocked off," commented Quinny. "In a lousy China-town basement."

"Funny for who?" demanded Honey Joe. "Not me. And not him."

"I mean this is about the last place I'd ever have looked for Austen. Those Fifty-second Street birds never fly this far south."

"Well, this one did," replied Hix, eyeing the ceiling as though mildly surprised to find it still in place. "And he brought more of them along with him. Only a little while ago he comes stalking in here with some other gents and some lady-birds, too."

"Dressed up like bums?" asked Quinny, wondering if it had been some sort of masquerade party.

"Not my kind of bums," answered Hix, contemptuously. "Evening clothes, all of 'em, includin' him. I didn't waste much time on 'em—they just came to wisecrack, just for a gag. No respect for the dump at all. I eased 'em along into the Joss House without showing 'em the Ladies' Parlor. They didn't like the Joss House, either—one of the dames squawked because incense smoke got in her nose, stuff that I pay fourteen cents a pound for. Sacrilegious, she was."

Quinny sniffed. "That what I smell now?"

"Yeah," affirmed Hix. "It's the real McCoy—all Chinese temples use it, they tell me. Well, anyhow, after they didn't like the Joss House, I shooed 'em into the elevator to go upstairs to Chungking Garden. That's the restaurant on the top floor—fancy enough even for these eggs."

"Did all of 'em go upstairs?" asked Quinny. "Or did this man stay behind?"

"They all went—eight of them. I noticed him particular, on account of him being so damned high-hat."

"You didn't see him again after they went up?"

"Not till just now. None of them."

Quinny sent Hix to keep his zombies in the Ladies' Parlor, warning him to make sure none of them got out. The dive had a telephone, concealed in a closet, used mainly to keep Hix informed of the departure of Chinatown buses from Times Square. These didn't leave on any schedule, but whenever enough sightseers had purchased tickets. After a moment's reflection, Quinny called his favorite newspaper, the *Observer*, making a satisfactory deal for exclusive news of sensational proportions. He then called Inspector Pierson, his old boss, at Police Headquarters, a few blocks away on Center Street.

"Got a nice, fat murder job for you, Chief," said Quinny when he recognized Pierson's voice on the phone. "I can see your picture in the paper again right now. After I get done cracking the case for you."

"Oh, yeah?" snorted Inspector Pierson. "Well, I don't see you on the short end, either. Come on—out with it."

Quinny explained briefly and then listened to Pierson's instructions, nodding his head at the proper places, even though Pierson couldn't see him. Then he hung up the phone and came out. He returned to the bunk, where he stood looking at the body, his new derby pushed back and one hand thrust deep into a hip pocket. One of the most curious murder setups he'd come across, he decided. Rich playboy in a tramp's outfit, dead in a bunk in a phony opium den.

Ignoring all the rules, he gave the body a cursory examination. The coat pockets were empty, except for a small cardboard box, labeled *Nolikker*. The detective recognized the preparation as one designed to stop the drink habit, but more often used by bartenders in less refined groggeries as a ready-made Mickey Finn. Its effect, when the powder was dissolved in a drink, was to make the drinker violently sick within a few minutes after taking. Quinny didn't think any Bowery derelict was likely to carry them around for self-administration.

An uproar in Doyers Street caused by arriving cars from Police Headquarters heralded the arrival of Inspector Pierson and his crew of murder men. Quinny retreated to the table in the center of the room and sat on it. He adjusted himself to look as if he had been sitting on the table for a long, long time—and getting pretty bored with it. Inspector Pierson heaved into sight in the doorway, other tramping feet sounding behind him.

"Hello, Hite," he greeted, looking around him. "What have we here?"

Quinny jerked his head in the direction of the bunk.

"There in the shelf," he said, sliding off the table. "Where'd you go after I called you—for a ride in the park?" One of the nice things about being a private detective was that you didn't have to be too respectful toward the brass hats of the force. There was a point, though, easily recognized by Quinny, where you laid off.

Pierson took no notice of Quinny's impertinence, but walked over to the bunk, leaning forward for a better view.

"H'm," he grunted. "Dead all right. What makes you think it's murder? Another thing, Quinny, if you've got me out to investigate the killing of some hobo, well—"

"I didn't," Quinny assured his ex-chief. "I took a look after I called you. That guy is Tony Austen. You know, the fella who's always got his mug in the tabs—with some dame—and both of 'em with a drink in the mitt and a grin for the birdie. He's no bum."

"I don't see much difference," philosophized the Inspector. "A bum with dough is just the same as one that hasn't."

"They don't think so," returned Quinny. "Neither do you. You'll work on this case just as though Austen was a silk hat from City Hall. So will I—I think. Might be a piece of this here oblong money in it, at that."

Quinny gave Inspector Pierson an account of what

he had learned, little as it was. After a brief examination, the inspector turned the body over to the department experts and went with Quinny through the doorway near one end of the bunk on a tour of the basement. This door opened into a narrow hallway and almost opposite was another door, the entrance to the Joss House.

The Joss House was merely a large room, somewhat longer than it was wide, badly lighted and heavy with the odor of Hix's bargain-basement incense. A gilded railing extended across one end of the room and beyond this was a large statue of *Chang-o*, the Chinese moon deity, glowing phosphorescently in the pale light of the place. Just a fancy statue to Quinny. But the thing was weird, with curling wisps of incense smoke rising from the holders at the statue's feet.

Behind the statue Quinny found another room, small, windowless, and bare, lighted by a naked incandescent hanging by a drop cord from the ceiling. This was evidently the room used by Hix's *Esquire* hired men to change in, as two seedy outfits of clothing hung from nails in the wall. Further exploration developed nothing more interesting than a small can of greenish paint spilled on the dirty floor. Quinny rejoined Pierson, who was standing before *Chang-o,* staring at it with an awed expression quite new to the detective.

"You know, Hite," he said, as Quinny came from around in back of the statue, "this idol gives me the woo-woos—kinda. Looks like it had been standing there staring for thousands of years."

"It ain't, though," replied the detective, practically. "A thousand years ago there wasn't any Chinatown in

New York."

Pierson's cold gray eyes swung around to the detective.

"Somebody told you," he said. "You never found *that* out all by yourself. Come on, let's see what else they've got down here."

They returned to the bunk room—the room Hix referred to as the "smoking lóunge"—where they found the medical examiner at work. Quinny was interested in several long smears of what appeared to be grime-impregnated grease on the stripped playboy's body, similar to the stuff on his face, but not deliberately smudged on as the latter had been.

"What's that stuff that looks like grease, Doc?" he asked.

The medical examiner glanced sideways up at the detective. "Grease," he said, succinctly.

"That's what I thought," replied Quinny, nodding.

"I don't suppose you've got anything to tell me yet, Doc," said Pierson, glowering at the corpse as though Tony Austen had kept him from something important—or interesting.

"Not much," answered the doctor. "Stab wound—almost instantly fatal. These rags were put on him afterward. So were these grease marks—you can see how they smeared the blood."

"Then he most likely wasn't killed in that bunk."

"I think not," affirmed the doctor. "There are no bloodstains in the bunk at all—on a superficial examination. Your experts can check on that."

Pierson caught sight of the deeply concerned face of Honey Joe in the doorway to the Ladies' Parlor. "Who are you?" he bellowed. The divekeeper took a step backward.

"That's Hix—the guy that owns the dump," said Quinny. "He's okay. I've known him since I was a kid."

"Then I ought to lock him up right now," growled the inspector. "What do you know about this, Hix?" He started across the room toward Honey Joe.

"I don't know anything at all about it," disclaimed Hix, hurriedly. "The man was a stranger to me."

Pierson knitted his heavy brows and nodded. "I guess he would be," he said. "What have you got in that room?"

Hix explained the Ladies' Parlor, and Pierson, followed by Quinny, went in to see what it looked like. It wasn't much like anything either had ever seen before. Apparently the room had been furnished in the plush era and never renewed. There was quite a gathering of Hix's synthetic opium addicts, still eating. Neither snow nor sleet nor murder nor anything else would ever give pause to their appetites. *Eat, drink and be merry*—Bowery philosophy runs—*for tomorrow the chances are you won't.*

Quinny observed that three of these men wore tuxedoes that had every indication of off-hour use for sleeping garments. There had been *two* dilapidated outfits of clothing—hardly to be rated as suits—hanging in the small room behind the statue of *Chang-o.* Ergo—Tony Austen presumably might have been dressed in the clothing of one of these *Esquire* bums. He pointed this out to Inspector Pierson.

"Then where in hell are Austen's clothes?" demanded Pierson.

"That's one of the little items we still gotta find out,"

answered Quinny. "The way I look at this, it's going to be a tough one."

"They're all tough, these fancy murders," complained Pierson. "Murderers are such damned fools, most of them. If they only knew it, the best way to knock off a man is to waylay him somewhere you know he's going to be, plug him, put the gun back in your pocket, and go get a cup of coffee some place. But these amateur killers have to put on a show. They got to make it big with a lot of trimmings to show how smart they are—and nine times out of ten something they do gives their whole show away."

Quinny nodded in agreement.

"Like the Ruth Snyder-Judd Gray case," he said. "And a lot of others. Whoever done this thought he—or she—was pretty slick. They figured that a guy picked up dead in a joint like this, dressed up like a Bowery hobo, would get a quick ride to Potter's Field and no questions asked. He might have, too, but for the fact that Quin Hite fell off a boat this afternoon and came to in the restaurant upstairs. Then I met Joe Hix on the street. Me and Joe went to school together, and he wants to show me his joint. We find the body. The corpse didn't fool *me* any—right away I see he ain't a bum."

"You mean that if it hadn't been for Sherlock Hite, the murderer would have got away with it," commented Pierson, sourly. "Listen, Quinny, you're a smart detective. I'll admit that, if it makes you feel good. But don't think for a minute that the murderer would have got away with this idea of passing Tony Austen off as a flophouse bum. He'd have been looked over pretty thoroughly at the Morgue before they sent him to

Potter's Field."

"Yeah," demurred Quinny. "And by that time the whole case would have been so cold you couldn't do anything much about it. When the homicide squad was lucky enough to have me on it, we missed plenty of times because we didn't get started until too long after the killing."

"All right, smart guy—now we're here and hot. Who done it?"

This stalled the detective for a minute, but for no longer than that.

"A half hour ago I discover a murder," he replied. "Now you ask who done it? I don't know anybody this poor mug knew. I don't know anything about him except what I've seen in the papers now and then. And you ask me, 'Smart guy—who done it?'—just like that. Chief, I think you are the wisest man on the squad, but I don't think you figure anyone is going to be *that* much smarter than you are."

"I don't," said Pierson shortly. "Thanks for the compliment, Hite. I don't think you are at all dumb, either. I wish you were with us, instead of fooling around with this private stuff—though you seem to be able to keep a couple of bookies on it. Let's skip all that. Have you any ideas how this Austen could have been got down here, murdered, and stuck into that bunk? I haven't."

"That's your big trouble, Chief—you're always in such a damned hurry. Let's just take it easy. We're only starting in on this business. Like you say, let's go to work, instead of guessing."

"Right," agreed Inspector Pierson. Probably there was no one the inspector disapproved of as thoroughly and still in his stubborn heart appraised more highly than Quin Hite, his ex-star detective.

Quinny eyed the off-duty dope addicts, who seemed to have lost some of their interest in the victuals provided by Hix.

"Hey!" he exclaimed suddenly. "You three guys in the tuxes—come on in here." He turned back into the bunk-lined room, with Pierson coming along. The three men Quinny had indicated shuffled uneasily in after them, lining up against one of the bunks and trying not to see the removal of Austen's body which was going on at the moment. The dead playboy was once more clad in the ragged outfit. Quinny halted the proceedings.

"Whose clothes has this man got on?" he asked, indicating the still figure on the stretcher. "Which one of you guys?"

The trio stared. One of them gulped noisily. "Me," he choked. "Them's my clothes."

"Okay," said Quinny, cheerfully. Then, to the stretcher bearers: "Take him away."

"How about me?" queried the derelict, watching the procession with distaste. "What am I going to wear when I leave here?"

"Wear what you've got on," said Pierson.

The man glanced down at the shabby tuxedo he had on. He didn't seem favorably impressed. "Me—wear this outfit home?" he demurred. "Hey, cop, where do you think I live—the Waldorf? Can you see me walkin' inta th' Eagle flophouse in these duds? I kin hear George—that's the night clerk—askin' if I want the bridal suite—and do they have to furnish the bride—"

"Well, if that outfit's too classy for you, go naked."

This suggestion also appeared to be unsuitable to the Bowery person. Besides, he pointed out, it was raining.

"Chief, Hix tells me that when Austen and his party left here they went upstairs to Chungking Garden," Quinny said, abruptly. "I just came down from there before I ran into this mess and there was a party going on that looked like it might have been Austen's. Suppose we go up and see if they are still there?"

"Right," agreed Pierson. He ordered the tramps to be kept where they were and meanwhile a guard stationed at all entrances to the building. "Not that I suppose we'll find 'em all—these joints have more ways of getting in and out than Grand Central Terminal."

They found the elevator at the end of the hall leading past the Joss House. This hall made a right-hand turn to the elevator, and its only illumination came from three overhead light bulbs. The small elevator was pretty well filled with cops as it rose slowly to the upper floor.

"You said Hix told you Austen and his party went upstairs from this joint," said Pierson. "How do we know Austen did? How do we know one of those bums didn't knock him off, switch the clothes, and stash Austen's valuables where he could pick 'em up later? For that matter, your friend Hix could have done it himself. He's the only one that says Austen went with the others. Now, *that* makes a picture."

"Sure does, Chief," agreed Quinny. "Just needs a couple of holes plugged up before you turn it in."

"What holes?"

"Well, one is, how did Austen get all that grease on him? Also where? I haven't seen any in the basement anywhere."

"There was some kind of grease in that can of phony opium on the table," volunteered a detective from the rear of the car.

"Yeah, there was," affirmed Quinny. "I saw it, but it didn't look like the same stuff. Anyhow, why was it put on? I don't mean the smudges on the face—they was put there to make him look dirty. I mean the slashes of grease all over him—like he'd been dragged over something greasy."

"I don't know the answer to that one," replied the other detective. "Maybe whoever killed him rubbed him against something greasy while he was carrying him in."

"That's saying he killed him, took off his clothes, carried him into the bunk room, and put the rags on him," said Inspector Pierson. "Could be."

"But it don't fit good," demurred Quinny. "The duds we found on him were, according to what we know, hanging on a nail in that little room back of the Joss House. If he was killed in there, the murderer would have changed his clothes there, too. He wouldn't have carried the body into the bunk room, then come back for the clothes. Not with all those mugs scattered around in there. The idea would be to get the body into that bunk as quick as he could, the way I see it— and not leave it there naked while he went back for the clothes."

"You think he was knocked off in that little room?" asked Pierson.

"I think I don't know," returned Quinny. "But I'll say this—figure out how the grease marks got on Austen's body and you'll begin to have what it's going to take to crack this case, Chief."

Chapter Five

GUESTS AT THE GARDEN

THE ELEVATOR STOPPED at the fourth floor, as far up as it was designed to operate, and spilled its assortment of police into the foyer of Chungking Garden. From this room two arched doorways opened into the restaurant, while at the street end was a checkroom, a counter being mounted on the upper edge of a half door that could be swung in to afford entrance for employees. Between the checkroom and the building wall, a wide staircase led downward through the lower floors and to the street entrance. A pair of telephone booths had been fitted into the corner back of one of the openings into the main dining-room.

Quong Chee appeared in one of the arched entrances and, seeing the police party, came to meet them, a faint expression of surprise in his otherwise inscrutable eyes. He glanced at Quinny as though expecting him to explain this intrusion.

"This is Inspector Pierson," said the detective. "We got kinda bad news. There's been a murder in the joint downstairs—a man named Austen. We understand he was here with a party."

"Mr. Austen?" exclaimed Quong Chee. "In this building?"

"That's the idea," growled Pierson. "Know anything about it?" The growl was merely professional. The sinister, evil, and mysterious Chinese of one-time popular imagination doesn't exist in the mind of any New

York policeman, who knows these people to be the least troublesome of any element of the huge city.

"Mr. Austen was here, with a party which is still present," answered Quong Chee. "I did not know he had left the restaurant. What you tell me is distressing news, Inspector."

"You knew Austen? Before tonight, I mean?" demanded Pierson. He seemed to be somewhat amazed.

Quong Chee moved his head in that quick nod of the Chinese. "Yes—for quite some time. Mr. Austen is the owner of this building."

That anyone owned property in Chinatown other than the Chinese was an interesting discovery to Quinny. It might have surprised him even more to learn that very little of the real estate in this district is owned by its inhabitants, but is regarded as a very profitable holding by investors. As tenants, Chinese demand little in the way of repairs, pay their rent promptly, and give no trouble.

Pierson turned to one of his men—a uniformed cop. "Moriarity, you stay here in the foyer. Don't let anyone leave this place till I say so," he instructed. Then he faced Quong Chee again. "Where is Austen's party?"

"They are seated in a booth at the opposite end of the dining-room," replied the Chinese.

"You men wait here till I send for you," Pierson instructed his aids. "Come on, Quinny, we'll go visit these uptown barflies."

Piloted by the proprietor, Pierson and Quinny threaded their way through an area of mostly unoccupied tables toward the booth the detective had noticed from the mezzanine earlier in the evening. The floor show—a half-hour one—had come to an end before the police came upstairs, and dancing resumed. Austen's party was sitting around a table in the booth, not looking particularly amused. There were seven of them. Pierson addressed a tall and handsome man leaning negligently against the booth partition behind one of the seated girls.

"This is Tony Austen's party?" he demanded.

The tall man—Mayo Browne—stared at the police official insolently. "Yes, and so what?" he answered.

Pierson's cold eyes wandered over Browne. He shrugged. "So nothing—much," he said. "Just thought you might like to know that your host isn't coming back to the party. He's dead—murdered down in the basement!"

Mayo Browne's jaw dropped. One of the girls stifled an incipient scream, her eyes enlarging in horrified surprise. This was Fane Gordon, easily recognized from numerous pictures in the tabloids as the season's café-society glamour-girl-elect.

"Tony—is—dead?" she exclaimed in a husky voice that might have indicated too many cigarettes at too early an age. She recovered quickly. "Is this just another one of Tony's gags?" she demanded suspiciously.

"Ain't anything *ever* real to you dopes?" asked Quinny. "Don't you ever read anything in the papers except pieces about you and your buddies? Nearly every day someone gets murdered. Tonight—Tony Austen."

"What happened?" asked Mayo Browne, ignoring Quinny and turning to Pierson. "Who killed him? And why?"

"We are asking you," replied Inspector Pierson. "You were all downstairs in that phony dive. Start there and tell me what you did from then on. You—what's your name?"

"Browne—Mayo Browne," answered the tall man. "This was all Tony's idea, of course—the party down here. He planned it several days ago, for us all to come down on a Chinatown bus, see the sights just like any sightseers would, and then have dinner here. Later we were going on to Club Flamingo."

"You did that like you planned," said Pierson. "Except leaving here to go back uptown. You went through that joint downstairs—and then you came up here. All of you but Austen. Why did he stay behind?"

"He didn't." Browne seemed puzzled. "He came up with the rest of us. You see, I came down here day before yesterday to arrange for the party—"

"You said this was Austen's party," Pierson pointed out.

"So it was," replied Browne, unruffled. "But I usually attend to the details of Tony's parties. He is tied up with his business affairs during the day."

"While you don't have nothin' to do but cure your hangover," suggested Quinny. "Sometimes that can be an all-day job, too."

With just a glance at the detective, Browne continued: "When we had made the grand tour of the basement, we came up here. Eight of us. We sat here in this booth, where dinner was to have been served. This was just before nine o'clock, when the floor show starts."

"Then Austen went back to the basement after you sat down," asserted the inspector. "When did you miss him?"

"We hadn't been here in the booth for more than two or three minutes—I'm not sure whether Tony sat down or not. He said he had an appointment with Quong Chee, the restaurant proprietor, in the office on the mezzanine. Quong Chee, incidentally, is a tenant of Tony's."

Fane Gordon laughed discordantly. "Nuts!" she exclaimed. "That's what he said, all right, but what he probably did was go off looking for that redheaded Chinese girl. He had a yen for her."

"I wouldn't hold that against him," said Quinny. "But he didn't see her. Just before the show started I was talking to her myself up there on the balcony."

"I tried to persuade Tony to see Quong Chee later—after the floor show—but he wouldn't listen. He had been drinking a little too heavily uptown before we started out, and was inclined to be stubborn," Browne declared. "I didn't think—"

One of the girls laughed. "You're putting it nicely, Mayo," she interrupted. "He told you to keep your nose out of his affairs until you were asked."

"Sherry Gates, who writes a column on the *Examiner,* was sitting over there at that table by the door to the terrace," Browne resumed, with a sour look at the girl. "Tony went over to say something to Gates. I noticed this particularly because Tony and Gates had mixed in a fist fight last night at Club Flamingo. I was afraid it was going to start all over again, and was thinking I'd better be prepared to stop it."

"Gates, eh?" Pierson's cold eyes wandered around the room and came to rest on a tall but slouching figure standing at the bar. "That's him over there, ain't it?"

Browne glanced toward the small bar in the corner and nodded.

"What was the fight last night about?" asked the inspector.

"Something Gates printed about Tony in his column," replied Browne. "But they seemed to have patched it up, as Tony sat down at the table and Gates ordered drinks."

"That's news," observed Quinny. " 'Columnist Buys Drink.' "

"That's all," concluded Browne. "As it seemed they'd made up, I went over to the bar for a drink of Scotch. We had only *mu kwai lu* and *ng ka pi* here at the table, and I don't care for Chinese drinks. The show started while I was over there, and I didn't see Tony again. I don't know anything about his going to the basement, as you say he did."

"Any of the rest of you see Austen after Browne left the table?" asked Pierson.

"I didn't notice when Mr. Browne left the table," said a girl who identified herself as Peggy Long. Although smartly dressed, there was something in her appearance that caused Quinny to think she was not an ordained member of this group. "I left the booth here before Tony did. There is a Chinese painting on the wall the other side of the door where Sherry Gates was sitting and I went over to look at it. I saw Tony come over and sit down with Mr. Gates—I wondered about it, too, after the battle they'd pitched last night. Just as the lights went down for the show to start, Tony got up and went out on the terrace. He seemed to be sick—he had been drinking a lot. I watched the show for a few minutes and then Tony came back in. He seemed to have recovered—it was too dark to see very well—but I saw him enter and start across the restaurant floor, holding a handkerchief to his mouth."

"How did you know it was him?" questioned Quinny. "I was up there on the balcony then, and you couldn't have told Joe Louis from Jack Dempsey six feet away in that light."

"Tony was wearing a white linen dinner jacket," Peggy Long explained, "with a scarlet carnation in the lapel—one that Rita gave him uptown. He was the only one here wearing a white jacket, and I noticed the dark spot where the carnation was. Besides, there wasn't anyone else out on the terrace, because of the rain."

"What act was going on when he came back in?" asked Quinny, in an effort to establish the time.

"A sister act was just finishing. It was the first act to go on after the Chinese girl announced the show."

"My brother and I were on the terrace when Tony came out," spoke up a dark young man, glancing at the slight figure of what was evidently his brother.

"Who are you?" demanded Pierson.

"Dave Kelton," the youth answered. "This is my brother, Ward. We went to see if the rain had stopped —it had not—and then Tony came out. He went over to the parapet and was sick. Ward went to help him, but Tony told him to get the hell away, so we came back inside. He was standing at the edge of the roof next to a big urn with some kind of plant growing in it. I'll show you where."

"Later," said Pierson, turning to Peggy Long again. "You said Austen went across the restaurant floor after he came back in from the terrace. Where did he go?"

"He went on to the stairs to the mezzanine," replied the girl. "He stopped for a moment or two at the foot.

I thought he was becoming ill again, as he stood there holding onto one of the dragons at the side of the stairs as though he wasn't sure he could manage the steps."

"Then he had his back to you?" queried Pierson. Peggy nodded. "How was it that you could see him so well across the room when a minute ago you said you had to identify him by his coat?"

"The orchestra stand is at the side of the stairs—as you can see. The light was better there."

Pierson, after a glance at the stairway, grunted. "Okay—what did he do then?"

"He went on upstairs."

"Slow, like?" asked Quinny. "As if he was still kinda rocky?"

"No. He went straight on up."

Rita Camonez, another of the guests, spoke up, and said she thought she had seen Austen through the windows of Quong Chee's office—the windows overlooking the dining-room. She wasn't very sure, but had seen someone in a white coat cross the office and then, a moment or so later, someone else had crossed going in the same direction.

Rita didn't know who the second person was. Quinny did, though, on brief reflection. He had followed someone into the office after leaving Chinese Red, but hadn't found anyone inside. This must have been Austen, but what had become of the playboy after he went into the inner office? This might need some further looking into, he decided.

"Well," Fane Gordon announced abruptly, "I've had enough of this. I'm sorry about Tony, of course, but I don't intend getting mixed up in a murder scandal. Will you take me back uptown, Mayo?"

"He will not!" snorted Inspector Pierson. "Or anyone else. You are all staying right here until I say you
can leave."

"And who do you think you are?" drawled Fane,
with a rising inflection in her husky voice.

"Inspector Pierson, if you want to know," returned
the policeman. "And what I say goes!"

Fane shrugged an elegant shoulder and turned up
her nose disdainfully.

"That's not so much," she said. "I happen to have
friends who will see to it I'm not interfered with by
presumptuous cops. I'll make a telephone call and
settle this little matter."

"You won't do that, either. This is murder—and your
big-shot friends can't help you any." Pierson glared at
the girl as though he would have liked very well to
give her a good spanking. "From what I've seen in the
papers, you were engaged to Austen. Considering that,
you don't seem much upset at his death."

"I'm not engaged to anyone, despite what you've
read," Fane replied, her eyes sullen. She glanced
malevolently at another girl sitting at the table—Dee
Forbes. "I'm not a Park Avenue gold digger, nor am I
interested in acquiring a second- or third-hand husband."

"Just what are you hinting at, Fane?" demanded Dee
Forbes. She was very blond, evidently a year or so older
than the Gordon girl, and not quite as pretty, but
Quinny catalogued her as being a member of the same
social caste.

"I don't think I need explain," answered Fane Gordon, loftily. "You know very well to what I refer."

Dee Forbes's face was flooded with color, but she

subsided into a sullen-eyed silence.

"What's this about second-hand husbands?" asked Pierson, shifting his gaze to Mayo Browne. "Was Austen married?"

"Tony had been through a couple of marriages," said Browne. "But both his wives divorced him." His lips curled slightly as he added: "Profitably, I believe."

"Looks like there might be a widow in the woodpile, at that," commented Quinny. "Any of you gals here married to Austen? Chances are he's leaving a nice piece of change to someone."

Fane Gordon's feverish eyes rested on Quinny speculatively.

"You're cute!" she said abruptly. While the detective was framing a suitable riposte, she added in her insolent drawl, "Aren't you?"

"Understand this," Pierson announced. "I'm not through with you people yet. I don't have to tell you, I think, that it won't do any of you a bit of good to try to leave before I say you can. I'll be back here in a few minutes—and I'll expect to find you all within calling distance."

With a sweeping, glowering glance intended to impress the group, Pierson strode off toward the bar and the newspaper man, Sherry Gates. Quinny started after him, then changed his mind and watched the inspector as he crossed the floor and brought up alongside Gates. Gates looked around as though startled at finding the law at his elbow, pulling his hunched shoulders back as he straightened up. Physically, reflected Quinny, Gates and the late Tony Austen were well matched. He wondered who had come off better in the previous night's fisticuffs.

Chapter Six

NICE PEOPLE

QUINNY SAT DOWN at a table near the booth to review what had been learned of the incidents surrounding the strange death of Tony Austen. Of course, it wasn't his job. Private detectives seldom go around working on murder cases just because of their love of the work. Nevertheless, this affair intrigued his curiosity and he wasn't averse to whiling away an hour or so on it. Besides, he had found that murders involving people with money frequently pay a dividend to the solver of the crime, and in any event he had made a sale of news to the *Observer*. So far, he had little to add to the information he had telephoned to Parker, the city editor.

Glancing over toward the group sitting in the booth, Quinny caught Peggy Long staring at him. She smiled gravely and raised her thin, arched eyebrows meaningly, following this with a swift, sidelong glance at the others. The detective nodded at the vacant chair at his table. Might as well find out what was on the girl's mind. Peggy got up and nonchalantly walked over.

"Anything biting you?" Quinny inquired as she sank into the chair. "Like something you don't want the others to hear?"

Peggy lighted a cigarette from the match the detective held for her and blew out a thin wisp of smoke.

"Nothing, really. I just wanted to get away from the party—and you looked lonesome enough to buy me a drink."

"You want to be careful about lonesome-looking mugs which are willing to buy drinks," cautioned Quinny. "You'll likely as not wake up some day and find out your honor ain't where you left it."

"I don't think there's much danger of that."

"Well, I'd buy you a drink whether I was lonesome or not." The detective grinned affably and looked around for a waiter. "Also, I could do with a slug myself. Rye?"

"I like Scotch." Peggy smiled, and the detective liked the frankness of it. "I don't always get it, though."

"You know," he exclaimed in a chummy tone, "I never been able to figure out whether women really like Scotch or want it because it costs more. They used to get along all right with a slug of gin mixed up in yellow water they thought was orange juice. You know —prohibition. Surprising how the dames got educated about liquor right after it got legal. Didn't take 'em no time to find out which was the most expensive!"

"Perhaps I'd better have a glass of beer," countered the girl.

"No—you get Scotch. I wasn't talking about you. Just women generally." He hailed a passing Chinese waiter and gave him the order.

"What's your tie-up with Austen's gang?" Quinny asked abruptly as the waiter departed. "You're no deb, and never have been. Glamour ain't your dish, either. Glamour gals just glam. You do something else. What?"

"Thanks for the analysis," the girl replied, with a chuckling laugh. "You're a detective, aren't you?"

"So they tell me," admitted Quinny modestly. "One of the good ones, I hear."

"Well—I'm just a girl who has to use her wits to make a living."

"The hard way, eh?" Quinny removed his new hat—which Quong Chee had sent for to replace the smashed one. He rubbed a tentative finger over its smooth surface, then glanced up from under his eyebrows. "What do you use 'em on—the wits?"

"I dig up material for a couple of columnists, for one thing," she replied. "On the side, I plug a few gown and accessories shops to the night-club trade. People like those." She glanced back over her shoulder at the party guests, and her eyes returned with a wry smile twisting her lips. "Nice people!"

The waiter returned and surprised the detective with the information that the check was being taken care of. The surprise was refreshing. Quinny glanced toward the bar and saw that the little Chinese, Quong Chee, had joined Pierson and Gates. As he looked, Quong Chee smiled across the room at him and nodded.

"I figured you out as being some kind of a ringer in Austen's party," said the detective, returning to his companion. "I could see you didn't belong, somehow."

"I don't." Peggy Long didn't seem to resent his implication. "Of course, I know them all pretty well, but I don't as a rule get invited to accompany them on expeditions away from Fifty-second Street."

"What happened this time?"

"I just happened to wander into the cocktail lounge where they had planned to meet before they came down here," explained the girl. "Some girl that Tony had invited on this party didn't show up. So he broke down and asked me."

Quinny nodded understandingly. "What time did

this gang start down here?" he asked.

"It was after eight, I think," answered the girl. "I don't know, exactly. I asked Mayo Browne what time it was before we left, but he didn't know, either. He wasn't wearing his watch. But it must have been quite a while before nine o'clock, because the floor show here starts then. Tony was anxious to get here before it started. He was interested in that Chinese girl—Chinese Red, they call her. We were here at least fifteen minutes before the show started."

"You came down on a bus?"

"Yes—that was another of Tony's ideas, I gather. What a ride! The bus called for us at the cocktail lounge, and the eight of us got in. Not much of a load for the thing. Then we came sailing—bumping is perhaps a better word—down Park Avenue to Fourteenth Street and then through the Bowery to Chinatown. What a ride!"

Quinny nodded thoughtfully, taking a sip of his rye and soda. His own journey to Chinatown hadn't been orthodox.

"What's the low-down on these people—Austen and his guests?" he asked. "You know 'em all pretty well, I guess."

The girl smiled crisply. "Too well. They're a poisonous lot. Tony Austen, of course, was just a night-club smarty who thought every girl he met was on the make for him. I suppose plenty of them were. He had money, you know."

"How did he get it—this dough?"

"Oh, he had one of those things you hear about—a rich uncle. That was Anthony Barwin, who made a fortune in the Orient. He died some years ago and

Tony Austen came in for a big part of the estate. Otherwise, the lad would have worked up a career behind one of the better soda fountains around town. You see, he had been raised by his uncle and aunt. Mrs. Barwin, the aunt, by the way, likes her cut of night life now and then, although I'm not saying she travels in Tony's set. I wouldn't have expected her on this sort of party—the Rainbow Room is more her style. She and old man Barwin lived in the Far East for a good many years. Tony was with them then, of course.

"The pretty little bitch is Fane Gordon—this season's café-society glamour girl. She's a spoiled, swell-headed brat, but not really to be blamed for it. She has an aunt, too, who has made practically a three-ring circus of the kid in order to bask in Fane's publicity. The girl's whole life is just dinner, dance, and drink. It is all she knows."

Peggy Long went on to describe the others. While she seemed to resent them to some extent, her summing up was not too malicious, and the detective believed he was getting a reasonably fair account.

"Dee Forbes's father got himself out on a financial limb last year bringing her out. She's the blonde in the black net dress. Last year's glamour child, you know."

Quinny shook his head. These glamour children came and went too fast, and then he'd never been even moderately interested in café-society happenings anyway.

"Dee managed to get herself engaged to Tony Austen. For a time it seemed as though Papa Forbes would cash his tickets. But to become engaged to Tony was no great trick—getting him up a church aisle was the obstacle hard to accomplish. He ditched her for the new beauty—Fane. Dee's father took it badly. The newspapers had it that he fell from his office window—ten stories. Not many of us believe that it was an accident. He had gone broke financing Dee's campaign. She's been just a hanger-on since then.

"Another one who was upset by Tony's shift from Dee to Fane was Mayo Browne—the tall man. Austen's pet mollusk."

Quinny was no ichthyologist. "What's that?" he asked.

"Oh—a parasite." The definition was on the broad side, but the detective got the general idea.

"Leave out the hard words," he suggested. "I only speak Times Square myself. You mean he hung around Austen for what he could get off of him."

"Yes. Mayo Browne hasn't a dime he's entitled to, and the Fane Gordon enterprise was attractive. Before Tony changed his plans, Browne had been doing very well with Fane. But Austen cut in—Browne bowed out. He had to, since he couldn't put on the show that Tony could. It is also whispered about that Tony picked up a couple of bad checks bearing Mayo Browne's autograph, holding them for Mayo to redeem by his attention to Tony's interests."

"Nice people you go with," commented Quinny.

"Not *my* kind of people," countered Peggy, flushing a little. "With me, it is just business. That dark girl is Rita Camonez. She had been making a play for Browne. Her father has money, and the boy would be interested in that. The hitch is that Rita's father has a set of steel-bound requirements for his prospective son-in-law. The man must be in a position to invest in the old man's business—not that Mr. Camonez needs it, but just as insurance that the girl's husband has a little more on the ball than the night-club samples she brought home from time to time. Poor Mayo hasn't the entrance money.

"Lately, though, Fane Gordon seems to have been tiring of Tony's presumptuous airs. She's been directing her queenly graciousness toward Mayo again, putting the lad on quite a spot. He could use the Gordon bankroll, but unless he is sure of success, he doesn't want to let go of Rita. He couldn't play with Fane without all Fifty-second Street being aware of it, and then if she changed her mind again he would lose what small chance he had with Rita—and incidentally make a bitter enemy of Tony."

"What about those two little fellows?" asked Quinny, eyeing the undersized Kelton brothers furtively.

"Oh, the Kelton boys!" Peggy Long didn't seem to think them important. "They are about all that's left of an old Knickerbocker family. The Kelton bankroll died off before the family did. Both those little lads were out to take Fane Gordon at first, but as Dave— that's the older one—seemed to be doing better, Ward dropped out. They are just about as useless a pair of overbred Pomeranians as ever chiseled a drink in a Fifty-second Street night spot."

"Maybe having dough is a bad idea," mused Quinny. "This Fane Gordon's dough is doing her no good. Anybody can see that. And out of the rest of 'em, Tony Austen was the only one which had any. So he's dead!"

The girl seemed not to have heard this. She was still contemplating the unsatisfactory lives of her companions.

"I think the principal reason Tony has been getting

the brush-off from Fane was that he's been showing too much interest in Chinese Red. Of course, this girl was just a novelty to Tony, but novelty was the staff of life to him. One night he brought her up to Club Flamingo and was pleased as Punch at the impression she made. The Novatoff got all the notices—"

"The who?" interrupted Quinny.

"Her name is Sonya Novatoff. She's only part Chinese. Would you like to have her history, too?"

"Sure—if it ain't too long."

"She was born in Leningrad during the Russian revolution, of a Chinese mother who was the daughter of an attaché in the Chinese legation. Her father was a Russian official of some sort—possibly he was an Oriental also. He was killed during the upheaval, and Sonya—just a baby—came with her mother to the United States, under the protection of Quong Chee, who was in the Chinese diplomatic service himself at that time. Later Quong Chee opened a restaurant here. Chinese Red has lived with him and his wife since then—her mother died a few years ago. I don't know her personally, but the boys tell me she has lots on the ball—no pretty dumbbell!"

"The boys are probably right about that," agreed the detective.

"Well, she had all the lads crowding around at Club Flamingo, all right. Fane couldn't take it. She's used to being number one girl and nothing less. Since then I've noticed a marked improvement in Fane's self-control when Tony happened along."

"I guess," Quinny remarked, "the Chinese gal would be nice to hang around. Like my boy friend down in the basement says, she's a honey!"

"Incidentally, I have heard that Quong Chee doesn't take nicely to white men who are too attractive to his ward. Not nicely at all."

Quinny digested this while he finished his drink.

"That," he said, "will be something to remember."

Chapter Seven

THE HAND IN THE RAINCOAT

OVER AT THE SMALL BAR in a corner of the restaurant near the mezzanine stairs Pierson was talking earnestly to Quong Chee. Some minutes before, Quinny had seen Pierson apparently dismiss Sherry Gates, at least for the time being, and the columnist had drifted away toward the dance floor, where two or three couples were still dancing.

The inspector had not seen fit either to broadcast his business in the restaurant or to order the feeble festivities halted. True, he had been the object of much curiosity and speculation from the other diners, but so far they had no inkling of the gruesome scene in the basement.

As Peggy Long concluded her account of the backgrounds of Tony Austen's friends, Quinny saw his former chief with Quong Chee starting off toward the dragon-guarded mezzanine stairway. Tony Austen had last been seen alive through the windows of Quong Chee's office, and the inspector evidently intended to give the two rooms a going over.

"I'll be seein' you, Miss Long. Later." Quinny got up from his seat and started toward the stairs. "Thanks."

Halfway across the floor he heard someone call, "Hite—oh, Hite!" Without stopping, he turned his head and saw Sherry Gates walking toward the foyer with Chinese Red. They halted and Gates took a couple of steps toward the detective.

"Got a second, Hite?" the newspaperman asked.

"Shoot!" returned Quinny, slowing down slightly.

"Got any stuff on this murder you can give me?" queried Gates.

"What murder?" asked the detective.

"Austen's, of course."

"Tony Austen wasn't murdered," answered Quinny. "He couldn't stand his friends any more, so he committed hara-kiri. Look here, Gates—what did you and Austen talk about when he sat down at your table? After the battle you two put on last night, I wouldn't figure you were that chummy."

"Austen apologized, and we agreed to forget it. Disagreements like that are common enough in the night clubs."

"It's dopey," commented Quinny, starting off after the inspector and Quong Chee, who were halfway up the stairway. He didn't intend to miss anything that might develop in the offices.

Sherry Gates watched the detective's retreating figure for a moment, then turned to Chinese Red. "Slick guy!" he said loftily.

Quinny caught up with Pierson and the Chinese as they were entering the outer office. The inspector looked inquisitively at the detective and asked him what he'd been doing. Quinny answered that he had been getting the low-down on Austen's pals from Peggy Long.

"When you're working on a case like this one," he said, "it's a good idea to find out who the victim's friends are and what he's been doing to 'em."

"That's routine," snapped Pierson, who didn't want any lessons on police work.

"Sure," agreed Quinny. "But I wasn't doing anything else, so I thought I might just as well work on it while I had a good chance. That Peggy Long dame knows more about Austen's buddies than they do themselves. More'n they think anybody else knows, anyhow. From what she tells me, nearly any of them would have played his exit music with what my girl friend calls gusto. Do you know gusto?"

"I'll talk to Miss Long later." Pierson smiled grimly.

"You only think you will," contradicted the detective. "She does the talking. All you do is drop in the coin. I bought her a drink and she did a good ten minutes on it. Both sides of the record." He glanced at Quong Chee. "I mean the house bought the drink. Thanks."

"All right." Pierson turned away impatiently. "Let's look over these offices. Here's where Austen was last seen alive."

Quinny explained what he had noticed at the time he had been on the mezzanine after leaving Quong Chee's apartment earlier in the evening. Since he had entered this outside office immediately behind the man they now supposed was the late playboy, there wasn't much use in trying to find anything there. He suggested the inner office as offering better prospects and they went in. As Quinny recalled it, he hadn't been very far behind when the man he'd followed entered this room. He remembered wondering at the time what had become of him.

"What's that up there?" demanded Pierson, pointing at the top of a tall bookcase leaning against the wall. It appeared to be a bundle of clothing, and Quinny, using a chair to stand on, got it down.

"You hit the jackpot, Chief!" he exclaimed, unrolling the bundle. It was a white evening jacket. "Austen's coat."

Over the breast pocket was an ugly red stain. Quinny carefully examined the garment, which, aside from a few wrinkles and a wet right sleeve, was in good condition. He raised his eyebrows, then turned to the inspector, who was regarding Quong Chee accusingly.

"Anything to say about this?" demanded Pierson.

The Chinese showed fright, Quinny thought. His eyes moved jerkily from the garment to Pierson's face and then back. He spread his hands, palms upward, helplessly.

"What shall I say?" he asked. "I did not know of this coat you have found. I have not, as a matter of fact, been in these offices since Mr. Austen's party arrived."

Quinny looked at the disturbed Chinese curiously. If it had not been Quong Chee he had seen entering the offices, it must have been Tony Austen. The Chinese also wore a white coat—similar to a waiter's jacket—but he was a much smaller man. The detective, however, said nothing, shifting attention to Pierson, who was chewing on his lower lip.

"Where were you all the time after they got here?" the inspector demanded abruptly.

"I met the party in the foyer downstairs and saw them to the booth I had reserved for them," answered Quong Chee, his voice now steadier. "Then I went to the kitchens to order served the specially prepared dinner Mr. Browne had ordered a couple of days ago. I stayed in the kitchens until the floor show started, then returned to the foyer. Mr. Austen had said when he arrived that he wished to see me on a matter of business. I waited for some time, but he did not come to the foyer."

"You and Austen," put in Quinny, "did you always stage your business meetings in your office? Or did you usually meet uptown somewhere?"

"Mr. Austen has always come to my office, for some reason. As a rule, he telephoned me that he was coming down here just a short while before he arrived. I believe he spent little time in his own office—I was never able to reach him there. His real-estate business, I presume, required much travel about the city."

"You said you waited for him in the foyer," resumed Pierson. "But he didn't show up. Then what did you do?"

"I stood in the doorway to the dining-room watching the show for a while. There was a new act opening the show in place of the one I canceled last night." He smiled ruefully. "I found that I had made little improvement in the program."

"After that?" persisted the inspector.

"Why—" Quong Chee knitted his eyebrows thoughtfully. "I strolled around the dining-room, and then went back into the kitchens to see how the Austen dinner was progressing. On the way I noticed that Mr. Austen was no longer in the booth where the party was being held."

"Who saw you in the foyer?"

Quong Chee considered the question. "I think, as there were no arrivals or departures of guests while I was there, only the elevator attendant may have seen me."

"I see," observed the inspector. "Which means the only proof that you were in the foyer has to come from one of your Chinese help. And you Chinese stick together tighter'n flypaper when one of you is in trouble."

Quong Chee smiled. "A characteristic I have noted among groups of all nationalities residing in countries other than their own. But since your opinion of us as witnesses against each other is a common one, don't you think I might have arranged for a more satisfying alibi if I were concerned in this?"

"That might not be so easy," dissented Pierson. "Right now, it's clear enough to me that if you didn't kill Austen yourself, you probably had a hand in the arrangements. Come on in here and sit down. You've got a lot more explaining to do." Pierson strode into the outer office, seating himself at a desk and indicating that the Chinese was to sit opposite.

Quinny followed them to the door, where he stood listening to Pierson's sharp questions and Quong Chee's answers for a few minutes. Questions and answers didn't interest the detective very much—unless he was the one doing the interrogating. He left the doorway to make a more thorough inspection of the inner office, where the clothes had been found. Crossing to the room's one window, he stood for a time looking out. There wasn't much to see. Just outside the window was a narrow strip of roof, perhaps four feet wide, bordered on the farther side by the parapet of the front wall of the building. Streaks of rain coursed down the window pane.

As the detective turned to pursue his investigation, he heard a slight sound coming from beyond the door of what he had supposed to be a closet. He dashed across the room and yanked the door open, quite expecting to find someone hiding there. It was not a closet, but the entrance to a narrow stairway leading down into the checkroom on the floor below. He had been wondering why, if the Chinese had made an appointment to meet Austen in his office, he had waited for him in the foyer, which was diagonally across the dining-room from the mezzanine stairway. The answer, he thought, was revealed by the existence of this unsuspected staircase. Apparently Quong Chee had assumed that his interrogators knew of it. About halfway down, Quinny reached a point where he could see part of the checkroom, with a number of coats hanging on racks.

A slender hand and arm came into sight, fumbling with a raincoat. The hand disappeared in a side pocket of the coat, then withdrew and vanished from his range of vision. By the time the detective had come down far enough to see the whole room there was no one in sight. He hurried to the counter to see who was in the foyer.

A woman was just passing through one of the arches into the dining-room. Her back was toward Quinny, but he knew from her dress that it was Fane Gordon. His first impulse was to follow her, but after crawling under the counter into the foyer he changed his mind. He looked around for the officer supposedly on duty here and finally saw him standing against the wall between the openings into the dining-room, seemingly interested in the dancing.

Returning to the checkroom, he looked behind the several clothes racks to see if anyone was concealed there. Then he searched the raincoat he had seen from the stairs. For the moment he thought it more important to see what Fane Gordon had put in the pocket, if that had been what she'd been doing. The hand had been empty when withdrawn, so he assumed that she'd either not found what she was seeking, or else—more likely—had left something.

The coat yielded an object wrapped in a woman's handkerchief. A short dagger—a hara-kiri knife—bloodstained, was revealed when he removed the handkerchief. The corrugated handle was not one that would receive fingerprints, although there might have been some on the blade.

Rewrapping the knife, the detective dropped it back into the raincoat pocket, then started back upstairs, his mind working on the significance of his find. He found Pierson still hammering away at the uneasy Quong Chee in the outer office. The inspector didn't seem to be making much headway. As the detective stopped in the doorway, he felt a draft of cool air and glanced at the inner office window. This window had been closed a few minutes before when he stopped there to peer out. Now it was open, the fine rain drifting in.

"Who came in here just now?" he called to Pierson in the other office.

"Nobody," snapped Pierson, annoyed at the interruption. "What're you asking me for—you've been in there all the time."

"No, I ain't, either. I went down to the checkroom—there's some stairs in here we didn't know about before. Somebody came in here while I was gone and opened the window."

There was the sound of a chair scraping on the floor in the other room, and Pierson came to the doorway.

"I heard the window being opened," he said. "But I thought it was you."

Quinny called attention to the stairway, and the inspector went over to look down its length. This didn't help him any, as from the top of the stairs all he could see was the stairway itself. Meanwhile the detective had gone to examine the window. There were several tiny white discs scattered on the sill that he was sure had not been there before.

"Where did you go—down there?" asked Pierson, coming back from the stairway entrance.

"At the bottom is the checkroom. I went down to see what was there. Then I came back." Quinny was holding out some of his discoveries for his personal use, if he went on with the investigation. "So whoever opened that window did it from the outside, came in here for something, then went out the same way."

"Hell, Quinny—it couldn't have been a minute after I heard the window being opened that you asked me who had been in there," objected Pierson.

"You can do a lot in a minute," the detective pointed out. "If you know beforehand just what you want to do. Suppose there was something in here the killer wanted. He could open that window, pick it up, and scram out again while I was coming up the stairs."

"I don't know how that fits into the picture I have about this fellow in there. I'm going on the theory that he's the one responsible for Austen's murder."

"Yeah—and all you've got's a theory. Come on, let's climb out and see where this roof exit takes us to. Unless your theory can't stand getting wet. Probably is already."

"Oh, yeah?" growled Pierson. "Well—one thing that

helps is that stairway you found. Kills Quong Chee's alibi, which was pretty weak to start with. If he was in the foyer, like he says he was, he could have seen Austen go up to the mezzanine and beat him to the office by these steps."

"He could have seen him just as good from his office windows," countered the detective. "And he oughta know we'd find the stairs sooner or later."

"Even so," argued Pierson, irritably, "there was always the chance that he could run up here, do the job, and get back to the foyer without being missed. But I'm not saying that he actually murdered Austen. That detail could have been attended to by some one of his employees better suited for the job. Quong Chee isn't very husky."

"Not husky enough to carry around dead bodies the size of Tony Austen," the detective agreed. "Coming?"

Quinny clambered awkwardly through the window. That's the only way anyone can do it. Pierson followed and they paused outside the window to scan the possibilities of the intruder's retreat. To the left of the window the narrow strip of roof extended along the front of the mezzanine floor to the left wall of the building. Several windows opened onto this from the mezzanine, but it didn't seem likely their visitor had re-entered the building through one of these. A number of Pierson's men were scattered around on the mezzanine waiting for orders, making an unobserved entry difficult.

To the right the strip of roof joined with that covering the checkroom. The ladder from the fire escape, rising straight up from the third floor, terminated at the junction of these roofs and suggested a possible way of escape. Quinny walked along the roof until he reached the ladder and peered over the parapet. There wasn't anyone in sight on the fire escape below, but he hadn't really expected to see anyone. The intruder would have had sufficient time to reach one of the lower floors long before the detective and Pierson came out.

"Let's see what's around the bend," said Quinny, starting off over the checkroom roof, with the inspector at his heels, turning up the collar of his coat to keep the fine rain out.

The top of the elevator shaft loomed up in the mist between the checkroom roof and the terrace beyond, but between this shaft and the steeply pitched roof over the mezzanine floor there was a narrow alleyway. Quinny found a small, iron-covered door in the shaft housing. It wasn't locked, and he pulled it open to see what was inside. Pierson, with a flashlight in his hand, joined him and they peered into the dark interior of the housing. Just inside there was a narrow platform, which served to support the motors and elevator machinery. Beyond this was the opening of the elevator shaft, now filled with the top of the car which was at the floor below (as far up as it was designed to operate). The cables which raised and lowered the elevator went through a huge steel pulley attached to a heavy beam at the top of the shaft, several feet above the top of the car, continuing thence to the motors. As a place of concealment it would do, but neither of the men could supply any reason for someone hiding there.

Beyond the elevator structure they found iron steps and climbed down these to the deserted terrace. At the time of the remodeling of the upper portion of the building for restaurant purposes, this section of the roof area had been paved and arranged for the use of those clients who liked their meals out of doors. It was about twelve feet wide and three or four times that in length, with a breast-high parapet enclosing its two outer edges. Three circular doors ("moon doors," in the Chinese vernacular) opened onto the terrace from the main dining-room.

"That big jug over there with the tree in it must be the spot Austen picked out to be sick at," said Quinny. "If it wasn't that he was seen afterward, when he came back inside, I'd say this was a damned good place to pull a murder."

"Or take pneumonia," growled Pierson.

Quinny eyed his ex-superior speculatively.

"Feel a chill comin' on?" he asked solicitously. "Maybe you better go in and get a slug of liquor. I could use one, too."

"I never drink when I'm on duty," snapped Pierson, starting for one of the moon doors. "You know that."

"The hell you don't!" disagreed the detective. "I've seen you. Anyway—this would be on account of you don't want to get pneumonia."

Female voices in argument came to their ears as they entered the restaurant. Chinese Red was leaning back against a table, supporting herself with her hands on its surface. Fane Gordon was giving a remarkably good interpretation of a little hell-cat, standing in front of the composed Oriental, shaking both hands at her.

"—especially from a half-breed Chinese!" the glamour girl summed up, stamping her feet as though about to burst into a rowdy dance.

Chinese Red smiled with contemptuous tolerance.

"Better a half-breed than to endure the handicap of

no breeding at all!" she retorted.

That settled it. Fane Gordon might be out-talked, but she wasn't ready to concede being out-fought. She swung her open palm at her adversary's face. Chinese Red moved her head just sufficiently to avoid the slap with a skill that instantly evoked Quinny's admiration. Also his assistance. Fane Gordon found her arms clasped from behind in a grip too firm to escape.

"What's all this?" roared Inspector Pierson, glowering at the furious debutante. "Ain't there enough trouble here already without you starting some more?"

"She called me a silly little sycophant!" exclaimed Fane, trying with some luck to kick the detective's shins. "No one can call me a sycophant and get away with it!"

"It wouldn't happen often," soothed Quinny. "Ain't enough people know what it means. Including me. Anyhow—skip it! Also quit jabbing my legs with your heels. What we want to know is what you were doing in the checkroom a little while ago?"

"Was she in the checkroom when you went down there?" demanded Pierson, angrily. "You didn't say anything about that!"

"I was going to, Chief, but, when I saw the window had been opened while I was gone, I clean forgot it," Quinny improvised skillfully. "When I started downstairs, I saw this girl fooling around with the coats hanging in there."

Chapter Eight

THE HARA-KIRI KNIFE

FANE GORDON twisted around in Quinny's grip and glared up at him in outraged fury.

"Liar!" she exclaimed.

The detective grinned cheerfully and relaxed his hold. He thought Chinese Red was safe enough now from further assault.

The girl caught her breath and went on, "Why do you say you saw me in the checkroom? I've never been in one in my life!"

Quinny pushed his derby back, eyeing Fane with the expression of a pitcher studying the next batter.

"Maybe I didn't, at that," he said. "I saw some dame's arm and hand. She was back of a rack of coats. But when I got down into the checkroom you were the only woman in sight. You were cutting into the dining-room from the foyer. Where were you lamming from? Besides the checkroom, there's only the elevator and main stairway and a couple of phone booths in the foyer."

Fane bit her lip and glanced at Inspector Pierson.

"Do I have to answer him?" she asked. Pierson nodded vigorously. "All right, then, cute. I came out to call up my aunt and tell her to get me out of this silly mess. That's all."

"My orders were that none of you were to use the phone!" roared Pierson.

Fane Gordon was unimpressed.

"I don't take orders from big, bad policemen," she said. "Anyhow, the drip you had by the door didn't try to stop me when I explained I wanted to phone."

"Moriarity!" exclaimed the inspector, exasperated. "Quinny, go get that dumb cop and bring him here till I tell him something."

Quinny nodded and walked over to the foyer arches, where the luckless policeman still was standing with his back against the wall.

"Chief wants you, Moriarity," said the detective as he came up. He decided to make a little hay on his own while he had the opportunity. "Say, you saw that Gordon girl go into the foyer, didn't you? Just a little while ago."

"Sure," answered the cop. "Said she wanted to phone somebody."

"Did she phone?"

"Yeah—anyway, I heard the dial workin' and then I heard her talking. Whoever it was she was calling wasn't in and she slammed up the receiver and came out, looking damn mad."

"She often does," commented Quinny. So Fane Gordon was not the one he thought he'd seen in the checkroom. Well, who, then? He had returned to the checkroom too quickly for anyone to have escaped from there to the foyer. On the other hand, he had searched the checkroom after his return without finding anyone. "Somebody must have been in there when I came out, then scooted up the stairs to the office before I got back," he mused aloud.

The patrolman eyed him suspiciously. "Huh?" he grunted.

"Yeah—the Chief wants to see you," said the detective, suddenly recalling his errand. "He's goin' to give you some hell for letting the Gordon dame use the phone."

"He didn't tell me to stop anyone from using it," asserted Moriarity, aggrieved.

"Don't say that to him," cautioned Quinny. "The Chief never does anything wrong. That's what he thinks. You just tell him you're a sucker for good-looking dames. He's over there."

Moriarity trudged heavily off toward the group containing the inspector. He didn't think much of the detective's advice and spent the interval before his arrival thinking up a better line. Quinny stayed behind, ostensibly to assume the duties of the post until the patrolman's return, but really to seize the opportunity to study the new development in the checkroom episode.

What puzzled him the most, however, was not this so much as the suggestion that things apparently related to the murder were still happening. With Austen dead in Hix's opium dive, his jacket in Quong Chee's office, and the knife in the raincoat pocket, Quinny saw no reason for the murderer continuing to be active. Of course, whoever it had been he had seen in the checkroom wasn't necessarily the killer—in fact, he didn't even think it likely. That had been a woman's arm, he thought, or, if not, a small and slender-armed man with his sleeves rolled up. About all it proved was that someone still present knew more about the murder than he did.

His reflections were interrupted by the return of Moriarity with Inspector Pierson, Chinese Red trailing them a few steps behind. The patrolman's face was a lot redder than it ordinarily was, and Quinny felt a twinge of regret that he had missed the bawling out. That, as he well knew, was something at which Pierson was singularly talented.

"You stay in that foyer, Moriarity," Pierson was concluding as they came up to the detective. "And what I mean is, stay there. Don't let anyone leave the building and don't let 'em use the phone, either, unless I say so. I'll be upstairs in the office."

"Can I go now, Chief?" inquired Quinny, facetiously.

"You can do any damned thing you please!" replied Pierson. He ducked under the counter into the checkroom.

The detective waited for Chinese Red, who had hesitated a little distance away while Pierson was talking and now resumed her progress toward them.

"Kid Novatoff!" he greeted, admiringly, as she joined him. "Baby, the way you took your head out of Gordon's range was good enough for Joe Louis. I was looking for you to jab with your left and follow it up with a right hook to the jaw."

"So I am Novatoff for you now?" she said. Her eyes were disconcertingly steady.

"I was just kidding," denied Quinny. "You'll always be Chinese Red in my book of phone numbers. I don't go for the Novatoff stuff. Too much like a by-line in the *Daily Worker*. Where are you headed for? You can't get out."

"I don't wish to go out," demurred the girl. "I was going upstairs to see what is happening to Quong Chee."

"Okay. Me, too."

They went into the foyer, crawled under the checkroom counter, and entered the narrow stairway, Quinny gallantly allowing Chinese Red to precede him. Before she reached the top step the girl stepped on her skirt and lost her balance momentarily. The detective caught her elbows from behind to steady her.

"Thank you, sir," she said, smiling back at him over her shoulder.

Quinny released his hold and followed her into the inner office, looking at his hands inquiringly. Then he glanced at the girl's jacket. It had felt quite moist to his touch.

Before he could ask her about it, she had crossed the room to enter the outer office where Pierson was snapping questions at the restaurant keeper. Quinny followed her in, his hazel eyes taking in the scene before him with alert curiosity.

"How you doin', Chief?" he asked. As Pierson had only reached the offices a minute or two before, Quinny didn't think he'd missed much.

The inspector eyed Quong Chee balefully, then sighed. "I'm making progress," he said. "This man is a tough subject, though. He either has an answer to anything I ask him, or he doesn't quite get what I mean. By the time I get it explained, he's thought up something."

"Perhaps I do not grasp your diction, Inspector," disclaimed the Chinese. "It is—peculiar."

"Yeah?" snorted Pierson. "You understand English, all right! Don't give me that!"

"English, yes," nodded Quong Chee. "Shall we finish our conversation in that tongue?"

Quinny, on the point of observing that this would impose a severe handicap on the inspector, thought better of it in time to restrain himself.

Pierson rested an elbow on the desk in front of him and cocked an accusing forefinger at the Chinese. "As I was saying, my information is that you and Austen have been having a knock-down-and-drag-out fight about your lease—"

"To which I have answered that no one has been knocked down or dragged out—"

"I know, I know!" interrupted Pierson. "I don't mean there was an actual fist fight—"

"Then why have you spoken of knocks down and draggings out?" queried Quong Chee, mildly. "As you may readily observe, I have not the proportions of a fighting man."

"All right—all right! Put it this way—you and Austen have been having a hot argument about your lease."

Quong Chee nodded. "I think that is the traditional relation between tenant and landlord. Universal, as well. The landholder desires a maximum fee, the tenant the minimum. I think it is rare that this situation results in the slaughter of either."

"Wouldn't do any good, anyhow," concurred Quinny earnestly. "Suppose a lug does knock off his landlord and gets away with it. He just gets another one that's most likely worse."

"You keep out of this!" Pierson shifted his eyes to glare at Quinny. "I'm having enough trouble without you butting in. I'm trying to question this man—and all I'm getting is an earful of real-estate business."

Quinny lifted his hands and dropped them in a gesture of resignation. Pierson continued:

"You and Austen have been having a—an argument, about the lease. You've got a piece of money sunk in this place—a big piece. Austen didn't ask you for more money. He told you he was not going to renew it at all."

"Your information is not exact," responded Quong Chee. "Mr. Austen was not unwilling to renew the lease. What he wanted was to form a corporation to operate Chungking Garden and to include another restaurant uptown. Unfortunately, this other restaurant had been unsuccessfully operated by some of my countrymen. It would have been impossible for me to agree to Mr. Austen's plans unless he was willing to compensate the former owners for their losses."

"Where'd you get all that dope, Chief?" asked Quinny.

"Gates told me." Pierson did not take his eyes from the Chinese. "You're telling me that you wouldn't take over the uptown place unless Austen paid off what the other guys lost on it?"

"That is partially correct. I did not, however, require that Mr. Austen assume that loss personally. His idea was that I contribute Chungking Garden for stock in his projected corporation, while his investment was to be the cost of refitting and equipping the other place. My counter suggestion was that the former operators be reimbursed from the corporation profits. I was able to arrange for this satisfactorily with my countrymen to whom the money was due."

"Due!" snorted Pierson. "I can't see what the hell *they* had to do with it—if they had gone broke trying to make a go of it."

Quong Chee smiled reminiscently.

"It was on that note our discussions always ended," he said. "I might add that Chinese business ethics are not as elastic as those of other nationalities or races."

"So Austen told you that when your lease expired you'd have to get out."

"He was, in your choice of words, merely bluffing," answered Quong Chee. "Mr. Austen had not the experience to operate a business of this kind, which he knew, of course. So of what possible use would it have been for him to close Chungking Garden?"

"There are probably plenty of others who would be glad to get it," argued Pierson.

"No Chinese would take a lease on it, and no one else can profitably operate a Chinese restaurant." Quong Chee spoke with confidence of knowledge.

"That's what you say—and for now I can't argue," conceded the inspector. "But here's something else: my information is that you have had quarrels with Austen because he insisted on taking this girl here on excursions uptown and making a show of her."

Pierson turned his head to look at Chinese Red as though to appraise her charm. Her color heightened perceptibly under his frank stare, but she made no move to speak.

"Once more Mr. Gates, I presume," said the Chinese with a sigh. "But must all disagreements be termed quarrels? I did object to Mr. Austen's exploitation of Sonya, who is my ward. Sonya, I may add, was not in agreement with me on this. It was her thought that these occasional visits to Mr. Austen's night-club environment should be classified as advertising for the Garden."

The inspector swiveled around in his chair to face Chinese Red, standing quietly near the door.

"Tony Austen was making a play for you, wasn't

he?" he demanded. "He wasn't satisfied with showing you off in the night spots. That was all right as far as it went, but it didn't go far enough. Not as far as he wanted to go." He swung around abruptly to Quong Chee again. "I didn't get this from Sherry Gates, either. When I'm looking for information about a woman, I—"

"You figure the best place to get it is from some other dame," interrupted Quinny. "It is—if you don't care much how true it is."

"Are you charging me with the murder of Mr. Austen?" asked Quong Chee. "Am I to be arrested?"

Pierson's wide mouth twisted in a derisive sneer. "I'm not locking you up, if that's what you mean," he said. "Not on what I've got so far. You'd be out in an hour after your lawyer went to work. But I'm pretty sure of what I'm doing, and I want to warn you not to try to make a getaway from this building."

Quong Chee spread his thin hands deprecatingly. "My wife, my business—my life is in Chungking Garden. Death alone can take me from them." He smiled, a little bitterly. "Or perhaps a policeman."

"Well, keep in mind what I just said," growled Pierson, getting up from his chair.

"I shall," replied Quong Chee, rising also. He looked at Quinny. "Mr. Hite, you told me earlier that you were a detective, and Mr. Gates later informed me that you were an excellent one—"

"The best in town," supplemented Quinny—and he really believed that.

"I realize that for the second time in one day I am in a difficult position, one from which I fear I shall be no more successful in extricating myself than the other. I am now asking you for the correct solution of this crime, with the knowledge that a true solution will remove me from suspicion. I will pay your fee, whatever it may be. Will you accept?"

"And how I will," agreed the detective. "Not altogether on account of the dough, either. I never knew many Chinese—but now that I'm getting acquainted with some, I'm beginning to like 'em. Especially you." Then he glanced at the girl lounging in the doorway. "You, too," he added.

"Me cwy lu, too," she said with the ghost of a smile. "You bet!"

Quinny had more in mind to say, but was interrupted by an uproar coming apparently from the foyer downstairs. He paused. They heard Moriarity's hoarse voice bellowing and sounds of a struggle. Pierson, with surprising agility, sprang from his chair and rushed through the inner office to the checkroom stairs, with the detective close behind him.

They reached the counter of the checkroom in a photo finish. Moriarity was wrestling viciously on the floor with someone neither Pierson nor Quinny could see very well for the policeman's bulk. He was on top. All but wrecking the counter as they dove under it at the same instant, they scrambled up on the other side and rushed to the struggling pair on the floor.

"What the hell's going on here?" shouted the inspector, leaning over and pulling at Moriarity's shoulder.

"I got him, Chief—I got him!" panted the officer. "The newspaper guy—makin' to pull a sneak!"

He got slowly to his feet, dragging the disheveled Sherry Gates up with him. This took a bit of muscle, as Gates was no lightweight.

"What happened?" demanded Pierson, lowering his voice somewhat.

"This guy sneaked past me while I was talking to—" He paused, suddenly confused.

"Talkin' to a dame," supplied Quinny. "Go on."

"She ast me something," explained Moriarity, and went on hurriedly. "First I see is this mug crawlin' out under that counter there. I nailed him. He's a pretty husky guy, too. Surprised me, or I would have downed him easy without all this fuss."

"Where did you think you were going, Gates?" snapped Pierson.

"I wanted to phone my paper," explained Gates, sullenly.

"There ain't any phone in the checkroom." Quinny nodded in that direction and saw Chinese Red standing on the other side of the counter. "Why not one of them booths?"

"Miss Gordon told me no one was allowed to use those."

"Never heard of anything like that stopping a newspaper guy," commented Quinny. Then he noticed a raincoat lying in a heap on the floor. "Your coat?"

Gates, with a glance at the garment, nodded.

"I was going outside to make the call and then come back here," he said. "It's raining and I didn't want to get wet—no telling how far I'd have to go before I located a pay station in this neighborhood."

"Yeah, I can see you coming back!" sneered the inspector. "I've a damned good notion to lock you up for obstructing an officer."

"He didn't obstruct me any—it was just that I was surprised," objected Moriarity, sensing a criticism of his competence.

Quinny picked up the coat, finding the collar and giving the garment a shake to straighten it out. Something fell to the floor with a metallic sound.

The bloodstained knife.

Chapter Nine

THE WALLET

PIERSON POUNCED ON THE WEAPON, picking it up gingerly by the handle to stare at the bloodied blade. Then he shifted his gaze to Gates, who was still looking at the knife with a bewildered, frightened expression.

"This does it," announced Pierson. "Last night you stage a battle with Austen and get the worst of it. Tonight you come down here and even up with this knife. Then you stash it in your raincoat pocket and when you think you've got a good chance you try to beat it with the coat. Nice going."

"That isn't so," denied Gates, licking his lips nervously. "I didn't know that knife was in my pocket. What I said before is exactly true. I was going out to call my paper—after all, I'm a reporter and it's my job to turn in the dope on a case like this. Then I was coming back to see what else was going on." He fished in an inside coat pocket for a cigarette case.

"Coming back, hell!" derided Pierson. "By tomorrow you'd have been heading for some place where we couldn't bring you back."

Gates struggled to light the cigarette, his hands trembling and making the chore difficult. Finally he got it going and blew out a mouthful of smoke.

"Wait a minute, Inspector," he said. "Use your head. Could anyone as well known as I am get away that easily?"

"Nicky Arnstein rode down Fifth Avenue during a

police parade when the cops were looking for him—
and got clear down to Center Street to surrender without bein' picked up," observed Quinny. "He was a lot
better known than you are."

Gates was looking at the coat still in Quinny's hands
and his eyes widened. "That's not my coat!" he exclaimed abruptly.

"Now you know it ain't yours," growled Pierson,
skeptically. "You brought it out of the checkroom,
didn't you?"

"Sure. I brought it out, but it's not mine." Gates
pointed to the label under the collar. "I've never had
one of that make. It's the same color—but not mine."

Pierson searched the raincoat pockets while Quinny
held it, finding the woman's handkerchief. There
wasn't anything else there but a quantity of tobacco
crumbs. He looked closely at the handkerchief, noted
that there were no bloodstains on it, then held it up to
his nose.

"What's it smell like, Chief?" asked Quinny, his
hazel eyes amused. "Noot de amoor?"

"Tobacco," returned Pierson. "But it's a dame's handkerchief. Not your coat, eh?" He turned to Gates.

Gates turned around and thrust his arms back. "Put
it on me—it looks too small."

Once the man had struggled into it the fact became
evident that it couldn't be his coat. The sleeves were
short for his long arms and it was very tight across the
back. He took it off again.

Quinny had been reviewing the facts he had accumulated, much as a card player selecting something to dis-
card.

"Look, Chief—here's something else I forgot to tell

you about that trip downstairs I made," he began. Pierson interrupted.

"Seems to me you're forgetting to tell me a lot of things. You ain't playing ball."

"I am now. Anyhow, when I was going down the stairs from the inside office, I saw somebody sticking their hand in a raincoat like this—"

"Who?" Pierson demanded quickly.

"I don't know who. All I saw was a bare arm come between some coats hanging on the rack, fumble with a raincoat, and then disappear. By the time I got downstairs there wasn't anybody in sight close enough to have been in the checkroom but the glamour gal. Women, I mean—the arm I saw looked like a dame's arm."

"Fane Gordon?" asked Pierson.

A drawling, female voice came from the restaurant doorway.

"Am I by any chance being paged?" Fane Gordon leaned against the side of the archway, a hand on her hip and the other engaged with a cigarette. A very nice pose—one frequently seen on the back covers of magazines carrying cigarette ads.

"I thought I told you to stay with the others in the booth!" snapped Pierson.

"Oh, you did, didn't you?" answered the girl lightly. "Well, if you think the others are staying there, you're crazy. I don't see why I should, if they don't. I don't see why I should, anyway."

"See this." The inspector held out the knife by its handle. "Ever see it before?"

The girl looked at the weapon carelessly. "No," she said, indifferently.

"No? How about this handkerchief? Can you identify it?"

Fane left the doorway and came closer to the inspector, then leaned over for a closer scrutiny of the bit of cloth. Squinting her eyes thoughtfully, she drew her breath as though sampling the scent.

"I think it's mine," she said. "Where did you find it?"

"You know very well where it was found—in a pocket of this raincoat."

"What makes you think I knew where it was?" asked the girl. Without waiting for an answer she continued: "I probably left it on the table at the cocktail lounge where we met to come down here. One of the men picked it up, I guess, and put it in his pocket."

She didn't know who the coat belonged to, or said she didn't, which was no surprise to the detective. Raincoats look so much alike. Quinny wasn't interested in the coat, anyhow, for that matter. Since he now believed the knife had been dropped into the pocket by someone who just wanted to dispose of it, there wasn't any particular point in discovering who owned the coat. It might serve to keep Inspector Pierson busy, though, while Quinny worked on his own ideas.

"That's a small coat, Chief," he suggested. "Think it could belong to one of them little fellas—the Kelton brothers? It's a cinch it isn't either Austen's or Browne's."

"I don't have to guess," answered Pierson. He was eyeing Sherry Gates speculatively. "I can make sure. Moriarity!"

The big cop ambled through the archway. Pierson gave him the garment, instructing him to take it to the party booth and find out which, if either, of the Keltons it belonged to. There seemed to be small question in Pierson's mind that it belonged to one of them.

"Gates, you stick around here," commanded the inspector. "I'm not satisfied with you yet. What were you doing down here, anyway? This is off your beat."

"I come here quite often," asserted Gates. "I have an arrangement with the proprietor to get publicity for Chungking Garden. Nothing much in it—a little cash and occasional meals."

"Then you know all the ins and outs of this place," observed Pierson. "Well, I think you've got something on your mind you're holding back, and I want to know what it is."

"You know all I do about this—and a lot more besides," denied Gates. "You know where to find me. Why don't you let me go? I have a living to make."

"You'll stay here. Your job will wait. I'm not ready to let the newspapers have this yet, anyway."

Quinny reflected that the *Observer* had an excellent chance of scoring heavily on its rivals with the news he'd already telephoned. There should be a nice little piece of change waiting for him when he got around to collect it.

Gates, though patently resenting Pierson's orders, made no reply. He thrust his hand into his coat for the cigarette case. Quinny regarded carrying cigarettes in a case an an affectation unworthy of a newspaper man. Or anybody else, for that matter. He watched Gates curiously as the man's hand reappeared. It wasn't the case he had come out with, but a small wallet of about the same size. The newspaper man looked at it blankly as though he hadn't been quite conscious of what he was doing. Then his eyes cleared and he hurriedly thrust the wallet back into his pocket.

He didn't put it away quickly enough, though, to prevent Quinny's noting the initial letters stamped in gold on its side—"A.A."

"Let me see that, Gates!" he snapped, holding out his hand.

"See what?"

"That wallet you just took out of your pocket."

Gates didn't move his hands. He scowled at the detective and said harshly, "I'm not in the habit of handing my wallet around to just anybody."

"I'm not 'just anybody,'" returned Quinny, shaking his outstretched hand impatiently. "And that's not your wallet. Give!"

Gates's eyes rolled around to Pierson, as though for support.

"Let's see the wallet, Gates," commanded the official.

Gates slowly took the wallet from his pocket and handed it to Pierson, with a venomous glance at Quinny.

"A.A.," read Pierson. "Who's that?"

"Anthony Austen, my guess," Quinny answered. "How's about it, Gates?"

"Yes, it is," admitted Gates. "Tony gave it to me when he felt himself becoming ill at my table. Said he had a bad habit of losing things when he was drinking and there were some things in it of value."

"What?" demanded Quinny. "Something besides money?"

"I don't know," returned Gates. "He didn't say—and of course I didn't examine it. After I heard about his death I didn't know what to do about it. Naturally, having any of a murdered man's possessions in one's pockets isn't a comfort—but I didn't know what to do with it."

Pierson had been examining the contents of the wallet.

"There isn't a hell of a lot of money in this," he said. "Not what I'd thought a man like Austen would carry around."

"That wasn't where he carried his important money," volunteered Gates.

"No?" Pierson raised his heavy eyebrows as he looked at the newspaper man. "Where did he carry his big dough? Not in his pants pocket?"

"No. He—" Gates hesitated. "I don't know, really. All I know is that he carried heavy sugar somewhere on him."

"Interesting," commented Quinny. "If you really know it—and not just think he did. The only way you could be sure would be to know where he packed this dough. What *did* he pack in the wallet, Chief—besides change?"

"Some papers and cards. The usual stuff. Don't seem to be anything important."

"Any canceled checks—or papers like that?" asked the detective. Peggy Long appeared in the dining-room entrance and Quinny looked at her a moment before continuing. "Must have been something important in it, or he wouldn't have turned it over to Gates to keep for him. If he did."

"What do you mean?" demanded the newspaper man hotly.

Quinny shrugged. "You answer that for yourself."

"There aren't any kind of checks in it," said Pierson.

"Canceled or uncanceled. You think there is something missing out of it, Hite?"

"If there ain't anything valuable in it, I do. If there wasn't, why give the wallet to somebody for safekeeping?"

"Canceled checks aren't very valuable," Pierson pointed out.

"They can be. But so far as we know, Chief, we don't have very good proof that Austen gave this wallet to Gates."

Peggy Long moved into the foyer. "Perhaps I can help," she said. "I saw Tony give something to Sherry while they were at the table. It could have been that wallet."

"Yeah?" Pierson's gray eyes searched the girl's face suspiciously. "You're kind of in the same business as Gates, aren't you? Digging up dirt about people to print in the newspapers? Wouldn't be helping out a fellow lodge member, would you?"

The girl flushed, and there was an angry glint in her eyes as she answered. "Sherry Gates doesn't get any of his tid-bits from me. And I don't pick up dirt, either—for anyone. I don't suppose I've had fifty words of conversation with Mr. Gates since I've known him."

"My acquaintance with Miss Long has certainly not been close enough for her to go out of her way to help me," chimed in the newspaper man. "If you think that, you're off the beam."

Quinny wondered if Gates wasn't a trifle too enthusiastic. He suggested they hunt up Austen's pal, Mayo Browne, and have him check on the wallet's contents. They found Browne at the bar with Rita Camonez. Browne had a Scotch and soda in his hand, but he didn't seem greatly interested in it. Rita wasn't drinking anything.

"This is Austen's wallet, Browne," said Pierson, handing it to the tall man. "Could you check it over and see whether or not anything is missing from it?"

Browne looked at the unopened wallet in his hand. "Where did you find it?" he asked.

"Skip that. How about checking the contents?"

"I can't help you there," said Browne, shaking his head. "I've never been that familiar with Tony's possessions. There have been times when he was drinking too much that he gave me things to keep for him, but never this." He handed it back to Pierson. "Sorry."

"He's supposed to have had a chunk of big dough on him—did he give that to you?"

Browne replied that he had not received anything from Austen during this party. The playboy, he went on, usually carried ten one-thousand-dollar bills in a wide gold band which he wore on his arm above the elbow, but Browne did not know whether he had done so on this night. Quinny was reminded that they had not found any of the small objects in Austen's clothes which a man ordinarily carries around. Austen's watch was also missing.

"Here's something else I've been wanting to ask you, Browne," said Pierson, stowing the wallet back in his pocket. "This Chinese who runs the place met your party in the foyer when you arrived and went to the booth where you were throwing the binge. Did you see him after that? I mean—say, in the next twenty minutes or so. Or after Austen left the table."

"As I told you," replied Browne slowly, his brows knitted in concentration, "I left the table myself shortly after Tony did. I came over here to the bar and stayed here until well after the floor show had started. But just as the lights went down for the show and Chinese Red started down the stairway over there, I saw Quong Chee come from the kitchen."

"Where did he go?"

"To the foyer. I followed along, a few minutes later, as I wanted to make a telephone call from the booth out there. When I reached the foyer, Quong Chee was standing in the archway, watching the show, apparently. When I came out of the booth after making my call, he had gone. I did not see him again until after I'd heard of the murder."

Pierson nodded, shifting his gaze toward the foyer, diagonally across the dining-room from the bar.

"Did he see you?" he asked.

"I don't know—probably he didn't, as he was in the other archway—not the one I went through."

"Who did you call up?"

"I made a reservation at Club Flamingo for later tonight."

"That's right, Inspector," Gates chimed in suddenly. "I didn't see Quong Chee come from the kitchen, but I did notice him walking toward the foyer."

Pierson shrugged. "For that matter, he says he was in the foyer when the show began."

"Look," said Quinny, directing his question to Browne. "When you saw Austen crossing to the stairs on his way to the mezzanine, did he turn and look back toward the terrace doors?"

"I didn't see Tony on his way upstairs." Browne regarded Quinny rather disdainfully, as though rating the detective unimportant.

"You didn't?" Quinny seemed surprised. "Le's see: You said you were standing here at the bar when the show began. You saw Chinese Red come down the stairs—with the spotlight on her?"

"Yes. I said a minute ago that I saw her."

Quinny nodded. "When the Chinaman came out of the kitchen, she was just coming down?"

Browne observed that he'd also said that.

"You were here a while after that?"

"A few minutes."

"You stayed here at the bar a few minutes after Chinese Red came down—you mean till she got through and the show started?"

"Yes. But I'd seen the show before, a couple of nights ago when I came down to make arrangements for this party, and I had the phone call to make. Why the inquisition?"

Quinny shrugged and pushed the derby back. It didn't seem to have the proper clutch on his head, so he moved it again. Then he spoke: "I'm trying to get the time schedule worked out. What was the act that followed Chinese Red?" he asked. "That will tell us how long you stayed—if it's all of the show you saw."

"I see." Browne creased his forehead in thought. "Three men followed Chinese Red, doing a knock-about comedy act."

Quinny pursed his lips.

"I guess you didn't see that opening act, after all," he said. "You know, these floor shows are liable to change the bill without notice. You can't count on the show you saw a couple of nights ago being just the same. A sister team followed Chinese Red."

"A sister act? Perhaps I have got it confused with

what I saw the other night." Browne made a gesture of indifference. "Does it matter?"

"You get confused easy, don't you?" asked the detective. "That show wasn't more than an hour ago—and already you have it balled up with one you saw a couple of nights ago."

"Well, what's the difference—I can't say that I paid much attention to the show."

"The difference is I'm trying to figure out when you left the bar," said Quinny. "Anyhow, I know now why you didn't see Tony Austen come away from the terrace. You weren't here."

"All I know is that I didn't see him," replied Browne.

"Did you see him, Gates?" asked Quinny.

"No, I didn't."

"You were sitting right there near where he passed," insisted the detective.

"No, I wasn't. After Austen went out to the terrace I went to the men's room."

"Who did you see in there?"

"No one. That is, no one but the Chinese attendant." Gates seemed irritated. "What difference does it make whether I saw anyone or not? Are you trying to fix an alibi for me—or someone else?"

"I'm not trying to fix up an alibi for anybody," answered the detective. "Not that there ain't people around that need 'em. Take you, for instance. Last night Tony Austen knocks you flat on your piazza. So, maybe like the Chief says, you come down here tonight to even up."

"You—" Gates's voice choked up and he didn't finish.

Browne laughed. "You certainly are a suspicious little something, Hite!"

"I don't trust anybody," returned Quinny. "I'm a nasty little suspecter when I get on a job like this. Just because I haven't found out any reason to suspect a certain guy don't keep me from doing it, either."

"You see, Browne," said Gates, contemptuously, "to be a detective you have to be a heel by nature."

"All heels ain't detectives, though," countered the detective. "Some of 'em write pieces for the newspapers. Then there's some others which are handy with a chisel. I wouldn't trust either one of you lugs."

Inspector Pierson thrust his huge frame between the detective and the other two men, a look in his eye advertising his intention of stopping an incipient fight even if he had to start one of his own.

"Drop it!" he commanded abruptly. "The first one of you makes a pass spends tonight in a cell—and that goes for you, too, Hite."

"Okay," replied Quinny. "I'd take a week in the jug for a good sock at either one of these birds. Only I'm busy right now and like my old man used to say, 'Business before pleasure.'" He snapped his fingers against the rim of his derby and walked off across the diningroom toward the terrace.

Chinese Red was walking slowly along the wall from the direction of the foyer. Quinny met her just as she was passing one of the circular openings to the terrace. He stopped her with a firm grip on her slender wrist.

"Look here, Red," he said. "You know I'm working on the job of finding out who killed Austen. If Quong Chee done it, well, I'll be sorry—surprised, too—but that's the way it will have to be, if it comes out that way. Understanding the way I feel about it, are you helping me, or—are you?"

"I wouldn't do anything that would injure Quong Chee. He is like a father to me," answered the girl, meeting his gaze steadily. "I will not help you prove him guilty."

"That's what I thought," said Quinny. "But you pulled something a little while ago which, if it gets out, will land the old boy in the hot seat so quick it'll make his head swim. You've been up to funny business —and I want to know about it."

The girl kept her unwavering gaze on him. "Funny business? What is this funny business you accuse me of?"

Quinny noticed a couple of diners at a near-by table staring at them with lively interest. They were within easy hearing distance, and the explanation he expected of Chinese Red was not something he wanted overheard. Tightening his hold on her wrist, he started through the moon door, towing her along with him.

"Come on out here!" he exclaimed. "I'll tell you what you've been up to—and then you can tell me why."

Chapter Ten

THE SCARLET BOUTONNIERE

THE DRIZZLING RAIN made the terrace an uncomfortable place for a conference, but also desirably private. Still clutching Chinese Red's wrist, Quinny towed her to a relatively dry spot under the overhanging roof near the iron steps to the elevator shaft. Then he turned to meet her questioning eyes.

"Where did you find the knife you stuck in that raincoat pocket?" he demanded.

The girl stared back at him without the slightest quiver.

"Why do you say that?" she said.

"Oh, don't argue!" he exclaimed. "You know damned well you put it there. I'm tryin' to get this killing figured out—and you're doing your damnedest to gum me up. Do you think Quong Chee killed Tony Austen?"

"I know he did not," the girl answered with assurance. "And particularly with a Japanese knife. That was a hara-kiri knife, you know."

"You mean the kind of sticker the Japs use to commit suicide with?"

"Yes."

"Why not use that kind—if he happened to have one handy?"

Chinese Red smiled faintly. "He would not have one—handy. For one thing, those knives rarely get out of the hands of the Japanese—they are practically sacred.

Did you know that a hara-kiri knife must draw blood each time it is unsheathed? This is so, even if the owner has to prick his own skin with it. Another reason why Quong Chee would not have such a weapon is that no Chinese would tolerate anything Japanese in his possession."

"Just tell me where you found the sticker."

"When you came up to the offices with Quong Chee and the policeman, I was in the inner room," she said, after some deliberation. "I went there after you saw me with Mr. Gates near the dance floor. I heard you come into the outer room and thought it best to return to the main floor. I started to leave by the stairs to the checkroom—and the knife was lying on the floor just inside the door.

"I picked it up, and then heard you and the others come into the room. I stood listening to what you were saying—I heard then about the discovery of Mr. Austen's clothes. As soon as everyone seemed to have returned to the outer office, I started downstairs."

"I heard you—I didn't go with Pierson and Quong Chee."

"From the checkroom I started for the dining-room, and then saw Fane Gordon in the telephone booth. I didn't want her to see me, so I hid back of a rack of clothes. Then I heard you coming down and thought it wise to get rid of the knife. You came down and went to the counter, standing there watching the Gordon girl as she returned to the restaurant. While you were doing this, I took off my slippers and hurried back upstairs."

"Then out the window," nodded Quinny. "And back to the dining-room, coming over the roof to this terrace. That's how I tumbled to it. When you tripped on the stairs and I grabbed your elbows, your jacket was all wet. Besides, you shed some sequins off the jacket on the window sill going out."

"You are too much for me," observed the girl. "But then, of course, I am not experienced in such matters."

"That's why you better keep out of it—and don't be going around making this business any tougher for me than it is already. That's plenty!" Then he chuckled shortly. "In a way, though, you did help a little. Maybe we wouldn't of found the wallet on Gates if it hadn't been for you."

"But you won't tell the policeman the knife was on the stairs?"

"I'm sorry you moved it," replied the detective. "You see, my little lichee nut, the more stuff like that they find in Quong Chee's office the better it is for him. Look this over: Quong Chee goes up the back stairs and meets Austen in the inside office. They have a big argument. He gets mad and jabs Austen with the Jap knife. He thinks things over and decides that if Austen's body is found in his office the police might get an idea somehow that he done it. So he stashes the coat on the shelf, carries Austen down to the basement, where he finds a hobo outfit to put on him. Then he dumps the corpse in a bunk in Hix's joint and scrams back up here. Either coming or going he loses the knife on the stairs. Does that make sense?"

"I guess that is what the policeman thinks," said the girl.

"Not when he takes time to think about it," denied Quinny. "No murderer as smart as Quong Chee would frame himself up like that, and why the real murderer didn't see this too is one of the things which gets me down. The guy *did* have ideas. Pierson's no cluck, either. He's one of the best murder men on the force. His trouble is that he's generally in too big a hurry to get results. I'm never in a hurry—unless I figure the killer's got ideas about killing someone else, and that don't happen very often. Not often enough to count in a case like this. Pierson hasn't got a single piece of direct evidence, and the circumstantial stuff he has isn't good enough."

"Why do you suppose Mr. Austen was murdered?" queried Chinese Red soberly. "He was just a young man with perhaps too much money to benefit his personality—a show-off, of course, but not really offensive otherwise."

"That's reason enough for some people to get murdered," replied the detective. He was peering through the gloom at the tall urn near the parapet. "I never worry much about motives, though, till I get some kind of picture of what happened. In this case, I ain't got one yet. Just a lot of bits that don't fit together."

"What is one bit that doesn't fit?"

Quinny walked to the parapet by the urn and leaned over to examine the gutter which carried away the rain water. The water wasn't draining away very fast, possibly because of insufficient pitch to the gutter.

"Well, one thing is we haven't any real evidence that Austen was murdered in the office," said the detective, rubbing his chin with the tips of his fingers. "Not the way I think, anyhow. There wasn't any blood spilled around, and with a wound like that there oughta been some."

"Where was he killed, then?" The girl seemed surprised at his statement.

"I haven't found that bit yet. Maybe out on the roof —outside the office window. One sleeve of his coat was soaking wet."

"What difference does that make—whether he was killed outside the window or in the office? The knife was on the stairway, and his jacket in the office."

"Why?" demanded Quinny, without expecting a helpful reply. "Why would the killer put the things in the office and on the stairs?"

"To make it appear that Quong Chee was guilty. Isn't that what you think?"

Quinny was dubious. "If that was the idea, why didn't he leave the body in the office, too—and let it go at that? Why lug it down to the basement and dress it up in the bum's outfit? He took a long chance of being seen doing it. On the other hand, if Austen was killed in the Joss House and dressed up to look like a bum so he'd wind up in Potter's Field without anyone finding out who he was, then why try to pin it on Quong Chee?"

Chinese Red suggested bewilderment with her shapely hands.

"The only thing I can figure is that he was betting on two different horses. That is, if he didn't get away with the Potter's Field idea—like he didn't, by the way— then he wanted to make it look as if somebody else— Quong Chee—was the killer."

"Then you believe it may have been someone who was Quong Chee's enemy as well?"

"No, not 'specially. He wouldn't care who took the rap, so long as it wasn't him," the detective replied. "Then there's something else. If Austen was killed up here some place, how did the killer get him down to the basement? Austen was no lightweight—he was a husky six-footer. The only way to the basement is either the elevator or the stairs. The fire escape is out—two men, even, couldn't have carried him down that ladder. One man couldn't carry him down the main stairs—not without stopping to rest a couple of times. Anyhow, to reach either the stairs or elevator he would have to bring the body from the inside office, through the checkroom and the foyer. That don't fit the picture I'm makin'."

"Why not?" queried the girl, listlessly. If Quong Chee was not the murderer in Quinny's estimation, then it seemed she didn't care very much who was.

"On account of he couldn't be sure somebody wouldn't come in the foyer while he was going through. If he had it fixed up with the elevator boy to give him a hand taking the body down, he still wouldn't be sure he wouldn't run into a lot of Hix's customers waiting for the elevator when they got to the basement." Quinny didn't add that if it was found the body of Tony Austen *had* been taken down in the elevator, Quong Chee's prospects would be considerably worsened by reason of the Chinese elevator boy. It seemed hardly likely that anyone else could have prevailed upon the young Chinese to help him with a job like this.

Quinny turned to go back to the dining-room and as he did so he stepped on something soft. He paused, looked down at the wet flagging, then stopped to pick up a crushed flower. A scarlet carnation. He took it to the circular doorway for examination in the better light there, Chinese Red at his shoulder.

"Austen was supposed to be wearing a red carnation like this," he said, recalling what Peggy Long had told him. Rita Camonez was sitting in the booth, and the detective abruptly strode off in her direction.

"Look," he said as he came to the table. He thrust out the bedraggled bloom. "Is this the flower you gave Tony Austen before coming down here?"

Rita examined the carnation, comparing it with some she wore as a corsage. These were an unusual shade of scarlet and matched the one Quinny had found perfectly.

"It must be," she said. "Where did you find it?"

"Out there." Quinny waved a careless hand toward the terrace and returned to Chinese Red, who had stopped by the table where Gates had sat with Austen.

The glasses the two men had been drinking from were still there, a highball glass and a smaller one—a liqueur glass—containing the remainder of the *mu kwai lu* which Austen had been drinking.

"This is the same flower Austen was wearing in his lapel," said Quinny. He eyed the glasses on the table. "And those are the glasses he and Gates were nipping out of. One of 'em was drinking that Chinese stuff you gave me upstairs."

Chinese Red looked at the cordial glass curiously, then stooped to smell its contents. She would have picked up the glass had not the detective prevented her.

"Mu kwai lu," she said. "You can tell it by its odor— rose petals. But this isn't the right color—it is yellow. *Mu kwai lu* is always white."

"Yeah?" Quinny bent over and sniffed. He wouldn't have known *mu kwai lu* from *ng ka py*, but he did get the scent of roses. In the bottom of the glass was a yellowish sediment. He scowled as he recalled the box of capsules—the Nolikker—in the coat of the outfit Austen had been clothed in when they found him. Taking the cloth from a neighboring table, Quinny spread it carefully over the objects on this one, then looked around for Pierson.

The inspector was still at the bar, apparently engaged in a futile effort to extract information from some of the Chinese help. To a man, they knew no English whatever, at least for the time being, and Pierson was raging. Quinny walked across the dining-room to the bar, noting that a police lieutenant seemed to be disposing of the various diners in whom they were not interested. The performers in Chungking Garden's floor show had gone before the police party came upstairs.

"Chief," he said as he came up, "I just found out that Austen was doped before he went out on the terrace."

Pierson's angry eyes switched to the detective. "How did you find that out? Who doped him?"

"Easy, will you?" returned Quinny. "All I know is that his glass on the table where him and Gates were sitting has got what looks like Nolikker powder in the bottom. I covered up the table, but maybe you better put your experts to work on it."

" 'Nolikker'—what the hell is that?"

"Supposed to make people not want to drink," explained the detective. "All it does, though, when somebody slips it in a drink, is to make the guy sick. Austen got sick while he was at that table and scrammed to the terrace, according to what we're told. You might also put your buzzer on that newspaper mug and see what he knows about it."

"You're telling me what to do?" demanded Pierson belligerently.

"Just suggestin'," denied Quinny, hurriedly. "Since you ain't had time to think about what I've been saying."

"Okay." The inspector seemed mollified. He looked around and beckoned to one of his men standing at the other end of the bar. "Nick, go find Sherry Gates and tell him I want him," he instructed. "Then go downstairs and see if any of the department experts are still there. If they are, send 'em up. If they have gone back to headquarters already—phone for 'em to come back."

Quinny didn't go to the table with Pierson, but joined Chinese Red near the entrance to the kitchen hallway. There were still some things he would like to know about the drugged drink, but nothing that he thought there was much chance of learning at the table. One thing that bothered him was his knowledge that victims of the supposed cure for the drink habit did not recover from its effects in the short interval that Austen apparently had. They were usually ill for some time.

"Hix told me that he fed his bums with leftover stuff sent down to the basement from up here," he said, when he had rejoined the girl.

"That is so," she said.

"Yeah. But what I'm interested in is not the chow, but the way it was sent downstairs." Quinny still twiddled the bruised carnation—something else he'd forgotten to tell Inspector Pierson about.

"There's a dumbwaiter in this hall—near the kitchen," answered Chinese Red. "Used for bringing in supplies, sending out garbage, and such. The food for those poor fellows is sent down to the basement on it."

"Show it to me."

The girl led him down the hall toward the kitchen, passing through a pair of swinging doors. This was the hall the waiters used in entering and leaving the kitchen. A Chinese kitchen man was in the act of loading the dumbwaiter with paper sacks filled with refuse as they reached it. He had more to load than the hand-operated lift could contain, so he was piling some of it on top.

"So that's it," observed the detective, eyeing the contraption with interest. The dumbwaiter was a shallow wooden box, with a couple of shelves inserted, and measured no more than a couple of feet wide by four feet in height.

"Do you think it possible that Mr. Austen was taken downstairs on that?" queried the girl, looking at the box with distaste.

Quinny shook his head. "No. It's nowhere near big enough to hold a man his size, even if it didn't have shelves in it," he pointed out. "If he rode down on top he would of had to stand up. Corpses don't stand up good."

Chinese Red shivered. "Don't!" she exclaimed, softly.

Quinny raised a hand deprecatingly and turned to a door he had noticed in the wall alongside the elevator shaft.

"Skip it," he said. "But the thing has given me an idea. The dumbwaiter, I mean. Where does this door go?"

"There's a stairway down the back of the building," she said. "The second and third floors have back porches—I presume you'd call them that. This opens onto the stairs to the third-floor porch. Then, at the other end of the porch, is another to the second floor. No one but the employees ever use them."

Quinny already had the door open and now he started down. After a moment's hesitation, the girl followed. The third-floor porch was dark, but dry, sheltered by a slanting, galvanized iron roof. The detective speculated for a moment on whether this roof could have been used to reach the terrace, but decided that it obviously could not. He walked along the porch to the other end, where he found the flight of stairs leading to the porch below.

Huddled under the stairs leading down from the kitchen was the figure of a woman dressed in a black evening gown, who watched with nervous eyes until Quinny and his companion disappeared down the staircase to the floor below. Then she ran lightly up to the kitchen entrance and vanished inside.

All unconscious of this, the detective with the girl close beside him reached the porch below. It was a gloomy place, its sole illumination coming from the light of one of the windows, where a group of Chinese were solemnly engaged in a card game. The musical intonation of Chinese voices reached them from adjacent buildings and the damp air was heavy with the strange odors of the quarter.

The detective stopped, staring at the wooden floor of the porch. A series of spots glowing dully in the murk were scattered along the floor and on the steps rising from the ground level. He looked around as though seeking the source of these spots, but aside from the window no stray beams of light were apparent. He bent over and touched one of them tentatively, then straightened up, frowning as he regarded his finger.

"Come on, let's go back upstairs," he said.

A creaking noise sounded from above, and the detective paused, listening. Someone was slowly and cautiously descending the stairway, as silently as it could be managed on the time- and weatherworn boards.

Quinny thrust Chinese Red into a space under the stairs, then crouched back against them beneath the railing where the staircase reached the floor level. Peering upward, he could see the dim outline of someone coming down step by step.

The descending figure reached the bottom of the stairs and stopped, his head bent forward in a listening pose. He was too far in the deep shadows for Quinny to get any idea who it was. A faint shuffling below heralded the approach of still someone else, climbing slowly upward. The detective hoped the newcomer would pass by without discovering either him or the girl, and was considerably relieved when he did so. Not that there was anything to be frightened of—the nebulous figure coming from above resolved into the unmistakable contours of Ward Kelton as he appeared on the porch. But Quinny, deciding the other shadow must be the brother, Dave, wanted to see what they were up to. Ward passed on to meet the other man.

"Did you find it?" one of the boys whispered hoarsely.

"No. There's a lot of cops in the bunk room. I couldn't pass the door without being seen—"

This was all Quinny heard. He leaned too hard against the railing and the wood cracked loudly in protest. Further concealment was useless, so he stepped out.

"The Hallroom Boys!" he greeted.

The Kelton brothers paused in their intended but unplanned flight and stared with startled and malevolent eyes.

"The cop!" one of them exclaimed.

Chapter Eleven

CANCELED—BUT NOT PAID

"JUST WHAT are you lads up to?" demanded Quinny, harshly.

Dave Kelton was the first to recover some part of his poise.

"We're leaving," he said shortly. "I went down to the basement to see if I could find a way out. We've other things to do than sit around a chop suey joint all night."

"What, for instance?" asked the detective, laconically. "If I was you two boys—and I'd hate to be even one of you—I don't think I'd go just yet."

"What have you to do with it?" put in Ward, belligerently.

Quinny waved an indifferent hand.

"Nothing," he said. He eyed Ward inquiringly. "Where were you when I left the kitchen hallway to come down here? You left after I did."

"I was waiting for Dave in the lavatory," replied Ward.

"Well, why didn't you wait?"

Ward glanced at his brother before answering. "He was gone so long—or perhaps I just thought he was—that I decided to come down and see what was keeping him."

"The men's room is right across the hall from the door to these porches," said Quinny, reflectively. He toyed with the idea that Ward had remained behind to watch this exit while Dave was downstairs, in order to prevent the latter being surprised at whatever he was doing, but since it was very evident that Ward hadn't seen Chinese Red and himself when they started down, decided the thought lacked confirmation. "Inspector Pierson will be interested to hear about you trying to pull a sneak-out. He is also going to be interested in how come you know enough about this building to use this back exit for your getaway. Maybe you better go back up and tell him now. Save you time in the long run."

"We don't know anything about this building," asserted Dave Kelton. "We just saw the door and thought it might be a way out. That's all."

"What did you go all the way to the basement for? If you was just trying to get out, why didn't you go through the hall on the ground floor?"

"There was a cop in there."

"I see." Quinny nodded. "Well, no use telling me about it. There's something else you can tell me, though. When you two guys saw Austen on the terrace —when he was sick—did you see anyone else out there?"

"No. It was pretty dark, though—there could have been others without us seeing them." Dave's glance flickered toward the top of the stairs. "Come on, Ward. We might as well go back."

The procession filed up the stairs and back into Chungking Garden. Quinny, the last to enter, caught sight of Dee Forbes in the kitchen, apparently taking a short course in Chinese cookery, under the tutelage of a moon-faced Oriental. The detective grinned and followed the others into the restaurant. Inspector Pierson, still at the bar and talking to Sherry Gates, paused to stare at the approaching group with the expression of a suburbanite viewing the arrival of unexpected Sunday guests.

"These boys had an urge to go home," explained Quinny. "By the back way. I told 'em they better come back up and get an excuse from teacher before they beat it."

"They did, eh!" Pierson scowled at the Keltons.

"I also told 'em you would like to hear about the back way out, on account of they seem to know all about it."

"It would be nice of them to tell me," said Pierson, frigidly. "So nice."

Quinny, however, seemed to have lost interest in the Kelton brothers. He saw Mayo Browne standing near one of the dragons guarding the mezzanine stairs. Browne was watching the group at the bar attentively, although he was too far away to overhear what was being said. The thing that struck the detective was that Sherry Gates, who had left the bar and gone around to the other side of the stairway, seemed to be watching Browne with just as much interest.

"What are you carrying the posy around for, Hite?" Pierson asked suddenly, his attention caught by the carnation the detective still had in his hand. "Planning to be a flower girl or something at a wedding?"

"No!" asserted Quinny, emphatically. "I been to one wedding today. It didn't jell. This is the flower which Austen was wearing, I think. I found it out there on the terrace a while ago."

"Yeah?" Pierson took the crumpled carnation and inspected it curiously.

"Mean anything to you?" Quinny watched his ex-chief's eyes closely. They seemed not greatly intrigued.

"Not much," replied Pierson. "I'll keep it, though."

"Thanks. I was getting wore out lugging it around." Quinny shot another glance at Browne, still at the foot of the stairs, and Gates loitering on the other side. "I see Browne and Gates are still at large. Did you put a quiz on Gates about the doped drink?"

"Yes. He says he doesn't know anything about it. He claims he ordered drinks after Austen sat down with him, and that if there was anything wrong with them, it was done before they were brought to the table. That fits my theory, Hite. The Chinese was somewhere between the kitchen and the foyer about that time. It would have been easy for him to empty one of those Nolikker capsules into a glass."

Quinny considered. "Yeah, I suppose he could," he conceded. "But there was two glasses. How did he know which one was for Austen?"

"Easy enough. The waiter would know which was which, for one thing. Besides that, Gates had been in the restaurant for some time—had finished his dinner. Even if the waiter didn't know who the Chinese drink was for, Quong Chee could have noticed what Gates had been drinking."

"You figure, then, that if the Chinese did the doping, no one but him, the waiter, and maybe the bartender would know about it?"

"That's right—and they are all Chinese." Pierson glowered at the bartender. It was a wasted expression, as the man wasn't paying them any attention at the moment.

"Okay. Now tell me why the Chinese wanted to

dope Austen," said Quinny. "It don't make sense to me."

"It doesn't?" The inspector seemed to think the detective unaccountably obtuse. "Look at 'em: Austen was a big man, the Chinese small. The shot of dope was to make Austen easier to handle."

"Nuts!" exclaimed Quinny. "Give a little guy a knife like that and the big fella nothin' but his fists and they're even up—except my money would go on the guy with the knife. Hell, Chief, if that was what was on his mind, he might just as well slipped a shot of some quick poison in the drink."

"You're working for Quong Chee," Pierson pointed out. "Naturally you're seeing things so as not to incriminate him."

"You know better than that, Chief," denied the detective. "You know damned well that I've never taken a job to clear anybody. If somebody hires me to clear up a murder, they have to take the chance that I might find out that it was them that did it. And if I do—they take the rap. You know that."

Inspector Pierson was forced to admit the truth of Quinny's assertion. At least, he admitted reluctantly, he had no concrete reason to support any other belief.

"Just the same, though," the inspector argued, "I think Quong Chee doped the drink. Why he did isn't apparent as yet, but will be."

"Another thing," suggested the detective. "There could have been other people at the bar when those drinks were passed out to the waiter."

"Sure, so far as we know now. But he would take care that they didn't see what he was doing. It's not much of a sleight-of-hand trick to dump the contents of one of those capsules into a glass."

"Two. Two is the dose," corrected Quinny. "That is, if you want to make a guy really sick. That reminds me—what became—"

"Two, then," conceded Pierson. "He could have done that easily."

"Yeah—but I still don't see why." Quinny shook his head dubiously. "If Quong Chee was planning to kill Austen in the office—like you think he did—why put stuff in his drink and make him so sick he couldn't go up there?"

"All we know is that Austen was doped, and that he did go up to the office afterward."

"That's all you know for sure—if you know that. Whoever doped the drink probably killed him. You can't ask for an indictment because you *think* Quong Chee put the stuff in the drink. You'll have to know he did—and so far you don't." Quinny contemplated the bartender, a slightly built Chinese, who now seemed interested in the conversation, although he had not volunteered any contribution. The detective addressed him: "Was anybody here at the bar when the show started?"

Pierson started to grin. He'd learned the futility of trying to question a Chinese. The grin died a-borning as the bartender answered in quite good English.

"The tall man of Mr. Austen's party," he said.

Pierson exploded. "Ten minutes ago you didn't know a word of English," he roared. "You learn fast!"

The bartender smiled blandly. "That was my brother you spoke to," he said, nodding toward a man washing glasses at the other end of the small bar. Pierson seemed to be having trouble with his throat. He gurgled inarticulately as the Chinese continued: "The tall man came to the bar and ordered a drink just before the show started—*mu kwai lu*. I did not notice when he went away again."

Pierson got his vocal cords in order. "Who else was here?"

"No one, sir. Few come to the bar, most of the guests preferring to drink at their tables. This really is a service bar."

"You didn't see your boss?"

The bartender shrugged. "I would not remember seeing him unless he spoke to me."

"That's natural, Chief," observed Quinny. "When you're used to seeing somebody around, you don't notice him much." He glanced up toward the windows of Quong Chee's office and saw the restaurant owner sitting by the desk. One of Pierson's detectives stood looking out through the window at the dining-room below. Quinny turned to the inspector. "Looks like you'll have a tough time proving Quong Chee doped the drink, though."

"Maybe I won't need to. I'm not depending on that alone."

The police lieutenant, Jack Madden, who had been interviewing the diners not of Austen's party, came up with a list in his hand.

"I've checked these people, Inspector," he said. "There doesn't seem to be any of them that could have any connection with this. Most of them are from out of town, with a couple from Brooklyn and the Bronx."

"For me, that makes 'em a hundred percent out of town," commented Quinny.

"All right. Get 'em out of the building, will you,

Lieutenant," said Pierson, scanning the list Madden had handed him.

"By way of the cashier's desk," amended Quinny, with an eye to his employer's interests. He'd often noticed that people are inclined to forget to pay their checks in a situation like this. "It's over there by the foyer."

Thinking of the restaurant proprietor brought to the detective's mind a couple of points he thought needed clearing up. This, he decided, was as good a time as any. Signaling Chinese Red to follow, he mounted the stairs to the mezzanine.

"Where do we go now?" asked the girl as she caught up.

"The boss's office," he replied.

Quinny surveyed the scene in the dining-room below. The Kelton brothers had taken seats in the booth next to the one assigned Austen's party and having in some way provided themselves with a pair of drinks looked reasonably settled. Both Sherry Gates and Mayo Browne were still loitering at the foot at the stairs, while Fane Gordon sat alone in the party booth, a turbulent and restless creature away from her customary habitat. The detective's interest then returned to the girl at his side, and he smiled down at her eager eyes, which had something of the expression of a child about to go on a picnic. This, he reflected grimly, was no picnic.

"I was thinking about Quong Chee's apartment," said Quinny. "So far as I know, Inspector Pierson has given it the go-by—"

"Oh, no, he hasn't!" interrupted the girl. "He sent men who examined it most thoroughly. Of course, they found no one there except Madame Quong Chee. I think Madame was of little assistance to the police. She does not speak English—although she understands it well enough."

"Why not speak it, then?"

Chinese Red lifted a shapely shoulder. "She is Old China, and considers that she can best express herself in the language she uses to think."

Quinny thought this over for a moment before replying.

"I guess there's some sense to that," he said. "I'd be in a hell of a spot if I had to think in Chinese, though. Come on, I want to see Quong Chee about something."

They walked around the balcony and found the restaurant owner sitting in his office, wrapped in Oriental calm. He glanced up at the detective and bobbed his head in greeting.

"Is progress being made?" Quong Chee asked. "Or am I to endure the indignity of being locked in a cell?"

"You're liable to," answered Quinny frankly. "Look: you said you waited for Austen in the foyer. What was the idea of waiting there instead of the stairway over by the orchestra stand?"

"I almost always use the checkroom stairway to come to this office," answered the Chinese. "I naturally supposed that Mr. Austen would join me in the foyer. I have always met him there when he came to my offices for business conferences."

"You did?" Quinny's brow furrowed as he considered this. "But this time Austen went up the other way? Why, do you think?"

Quong Chee shook his head. "I do not know. I have also wondered."

The detective stood in silence for a few moments, his eyes screwed up in concentration. Then his expression suddenly cleared. He pulled the derby down tight on his forehead and smacked the palms of his hands together.

"I think I get it—now," he said slowly. "I think I get it! All I got to do now is prove it—and that's going to take doing."

"Truthfully, I may say that I shall not enjoy being imprisoned while waiting the result of your discoveries," observed the Chinese, shaking his head dubiously.

"Most likely not—if it comes to that. I hear the service in the city clink ain't recommended." Quinny grinned.

Quong Chee decided that he would like some tea and food to while away the tedium of waiting, and asked the detective to send a waiter to the office when he returned to the dining-room floor. There was one standing near the foot of the stairs as Quinny came back down, to whom the detective imparted the instruction.

Mayo Browne had apparently wearied of standing around and was now occupying a chair at a table near the foot of the stairway. Quinny walked over and dropped in a chair opposite.

"Look, Browne—forget about us throwing hot stuff at each other a while back," he said. Browne raised a well-kept hand in a gesture of dismissal. "Tell me more about that gold band Tony Austen was wearing."

"What more is there to tell, Hite?" queried the man, wearily. "It was a band about an inch and a half wide and had been specially made to fit Tony's arm above the elbow. It had a lock, of course, the key to which he carried in a container with his others. This was a small key, and rather an odd shape—very much like a capital letter T. Besides the part that ordinarily goes into the lock, there were two prongs on the finger-grip to engage in the lock at the same time as the center piece."

"Sounds like something they might use to open up the Treasury building in the morning," commented the detective. "About all that means to me is that the key would be easy to identify. We ain't located any of Austen's keys, though, or anything else he might have had in his pockets."

"This gold band was what started the fight between Tony and Sherry Gates," mused Browne. "Gates got wind of it somehow—no very difficult matter, I think —and ran a paragraph in his column about the practice of a certain wealthy young man who carried a large sum of money in a gold bracelet on his arm. Gates hinted that it might be an excellent idea for someone who might be forced to leave town precipitately."

"You mean in a hurry, I guess," nodded Quinny. "And Austen didn't like the crack."

"He was furious. Gates came into the Bantam Bar at the Flamingo last night and without a word Tony socked him. It was a rare good fight." Browne's eyes warmed with recollection. "Gates tried his damnedest to brain Tony with a bottle. It smashed on the bar, and then Tony got through with a straight left and Gates went blotto."

"Oughta been a good battle," agreed Quinny. "They're about the same size. I don't see why Gates wanted to grab a bottle, but some guys are like that when they get hit."

"I wouldn't say they were very well matched, except

in size," said Browne. "Tony was huskier, and probably in better condition. He played squash racquets a lot."

"Ten grand's a nice piece of money," sighed the detective. "And it's most likely laying around somewhere in this place—or downstairs. That's if Austen was packing it tonight."

"I don't think he ever was without the band," said Browne. "I don't actually know, of course. If he wasn't wearing it tonight, it would be in his apartment and his man would know."

"Me—I wouldn't know what to do with that much cash. You, bein' in the bucks yourself, wouldn't understand just how much money ten grand is. Hitler started out in business with less dough than that!"

Browne smiled tolerantly. "I realize very well how much money ten thousand dollars is," he said. "You're wrong about me. I'm actually quite poor." He stared across the room with a quizzical expression playing about his eyes and mouth. Quinny turned to see what the man was looking at. It was the South American girl, Rita Camonez, wandering aimlessly away from the direction of the bar.

Browne spoke again: "My fortune is vested in a goddess—such as she is."

Rita Camonez, unquestionably a good-looking young woman, still didn't look like a goddess to Quinny. Goddesses, he believed, didn't have so much suggestion of zip. More calmlike.

"Here's something else." The detective turned back to his companion. "In the coat pocket we found on Austen there was a box of those Nolikker things. They're a kind of—"

Browne's laugh interrupted. "I know about them,"

he said. "Tony bought some once. He used one to make a Mickey Finn for Gates—among others. Tony, I'm sorry to say, went in for practical jokes."

"He did, eh? How long ago was that?"

"Oh, that must have been two or three months ago."

"Then it ain't likely this was the same box," observed Quinny. "Could be, of course. But there was only two capsules gone out of the box we found. Got a cigarette?"

Browne reached into a side coat pocket and brought out a package, tendering it to the detective, then fished one out for himself. Quinny supplied the match.

"How long do you think we'll be kept here?" asked Browne, glancing at the watch on his wrist. "I'd like to get these girls back uptown—especially Miss Camonez. Her father is on the fussy side when it comes to the sort of notoriety that will follow an event of this kind."

"I can't answer that," replied Quinny. "It ain't very often a set-up like this happens. I mean, where the police get on the job with the murderer still around and they don't know who he is. You see, it could have been almost anybody up here. Also, it could be someone who ain't here now. The inspector is busier than a setting hen with too many eggs."

"I wouldn't have thought you'd know the ways of poultry," smiled Browne.

"I don't know much," admitted the detective. "Most of the chickens I've seen was hanging up by their heels in a butcher's window, and you could tell by their eyes they'd lost interest in eggs." He got up and walked away in the direction of the terrace.

Quinny had been watching Rita Camonez. The girl had wandered over to the party booth, spoken a word or two to Fane Gordon, and then with a too obvious aimlessness drifted to the table where Gates had sat with Tony Austen. This table had been cleared of its contents by the department experts and left with nothing but the tablecloth. Rita sank into a chair, glancing around covertly as though to see if she was being observed. She didn't see Quinny until he had almost reached the table, or, if so, did not observe that he was interested in what she was doing.

She thrust her hand under the tablecloth and groped around. Quinny was at her side just as she started to withdraw her hand. He took her wrist in his strong grip.

"What've you got, sister?" he growled.

"Let me go!" exclaimed the girl, her eyes big with alarm.

"No! Show daddy what you've got in your hand."

She stared up at him with a hint of Spanish fury in her dark eyes, then reluctantly opened her hand to display two crumpled bits of paper. Quinny picked them up from her palm. Checks. Canceled checks, for considerable amounts, and signed by Mayo Browne.

"Collecting Browne's autographs?" asked Quinny, examining them. They had been made payable to Club Flamingo. "Funny, how the sucker clubs get taken by the suckers now and then."

"I don't understand why you say that!" the girl exclaimed. "These are just canceled checks. I don't see anything odd about them."

Quinny turned them over and called her attention to the backs. "These checks never got paid by the bank. That's what's odd. I'll take care of them."

"You've no right—"

"But I've got the checks." He thrust one hand into his hip pocket and assumed his most hardboiled expression. "So what? How did you know those checks were there?"

"I saw Sherry Gates put something—"

"What's wrong, Rita?" Browne had come up back of the detective to join them. "Is this fellow annoying you?"

Quinny laughed. "Yeah—I'm annoying her all right," he said. "She says she saw Sherry Gates slip something under the cloth on this table. Le's see: Gates says he went to the washroom right after Austen left him to go out on the terrace. When did you see Gates shove something under the cloth?"

Browne looked as though about to interrupt once again, but Quinny shot him a belligerent glance. The girl looked from Browne to the detective uncertainly.

"Before he went away from the table, of course," she said. There was not much conviction in her tone.

"Where were you sitting then—over there in the booth?"

"Yes."

"Which chair?"

"The same one I was sitting in when you asked me about the carnation," she replied.

Quinny looked over toward the booth, locating the chair. It was against a continuation of this same wall separating the dining-room from the terrace and just visible behind a narrow grille that bordered the opening of the booth into the dining-room. He walked over to this chair, looked back at the couple by the table, and returned, followed by the curious eyes of Fane Gordon.

"Who told you the checks were under the tablecloth?" he demanded.

"I just told you that I saw Mr. Gates—"

"Skip that!" interrupted Quinny. He turned to Browne. "Miss Camonez might be your idea of a goddess, but she's got only the regular kind of eyes. Gates was sitting here with his back to the booth. The show was going on, and this part of the room was pretty dark. She never saw Sherry Gates put anything under the tablecloth! Somebody told her. Was it you, Browne?"

MAYO BROWNE returned the detective's accusing gaze for a space before replying.

"Yes," he said, shortly. "I did. I had noticed Gates looking at the wallet—although at the time I didn't know it was Tony's—then shove something under the cloth. Later, when I was told who the wallet belonged to and asked if there was anything missing from it, I remembered what I'd seen. I knew, of course, that Tony had my canceled checks in it, and since they weren't there, I decided that must have been what I saw Gates hiding."

"Nice work," congratulated Quinny. He fished the checks from his pocket and handed them to Browne. "Here, take 'em. They ain't any good to anybody else—now."

"Thanks," murmured Browne, putting the bits of paper away.

"Where were you when you saw Gates stuffing the checks under the cloth?" asked the detective. "Not at the bar. You couldn't have seen what he was doing from there—not after the show started. Austen didn't leave Gates till the show began."

"That's right, but I didn't go directly to the foyer from the bar. I saw Tony feeling his way out to the terrace and started to come over to help him. I got about halfway across the floor before I remembered the Keltons were out there. I thought they would give him a hand if he needed it—I didn't suppose his difficulty was anything more than too much liquor. Then I saw Gates examining what I supposed was his own wallet."

Quinny nodded. "You stood out there in the middle of the dining-room watching him while Chinese Red was talking?"

"Yes. For a couple of minutes, I should say, before I went on to the telephones."

The detective reflected that Chinese Red had spoken for a good deal less than a minute. "But you didn't see Austen give the wallet to Gates, did you?"

"No, I didn't. The first time I saw it was when Gates was examining it."

"Why do you think he snitched the checks like that?"

Browne smiled cynically. "Knowing Gates pretty well, that's not a difficult question to answer. Sherry Gates isn't above a bit of picayunish blackmail, you know."

The detective didn't doubt this; in fact, it was the answer he would have supplied to his own question. The checks, however, had a significance for Quinny unrelated to the desire of either of these men to possess them. Gates's action in hiding the checks under the cloth instead of putting them in his own wallet was curious, too. Quinny walked slowly away from the table, deep in thought, his mind fairly wallowing in the disjointed strands surrounding the death of the playboy, Tony Austen.

He did not dismiss the possibility that it might have been Quong Chee who had committed or engineered this murder, but to his mind there was little to indicate it so far. Unquestionably, the Chinese had motivation and opportunity. There were others with possible motive. Whether these also had opportunity was still to be demonstrated. Certainly it did not seem so, if Austen had been killed in Quong Chee's inner office, as Inspector Pierson believed. But the detective was not in agreement with his ex-chief about this. He doubted that the evidence they had accumulated so far supplied indisputable proof of where the killing had occurred.

This is one of them cases where you got to start at the beginning and dope out what happened clear to the end before you go looking for the killer, he thought. *Pierson's only got a piece of the picture—and that was drawn by somebody else. Looks to me like the mug which done this was playing safe two ways. If he didn't get away with the idea of Austen being lugged off to Potter's Field unrecognized, then he fixed things so the rap would fall on the Chinese. That would make it look like it was somebody who thought he might get suspected otherwise. If the killer is somebody we don't even know about, it don't add up. He'd be a sap to go to all that trouble, if he coulda knocked Austen off and lammed without anybody knowing he was here. From the job he did, I don't figure this guy is that kind of nitwit, either.*

The only people we have to suspect are the ones still here. That ain't very many—outside of his party, and Gates, none. Yeah—the Chinese, of course.

Quinny eased his frame into a chair in the party booth. Fane Gordon was sitting opposite, with an almost empty highball glass before her, brooding and rebellious. The detective ignored her and went on with his thinking.

Le's see. Mayo Browne. He's just a hanger-on in this

*outfit. He ain't got any dough, and Austen bought up
a couple of his phony checks. As long as Austen held
the checks, Browne had to play ball the way his pal
wanted him to. Austen cut under him with this Gordon
dame, and he couldn't do anything about it. He can't
get anywhere with this Camonez child unless he can
promote entrance money with her old man. Ten grand,
if he could get it, would be the down payment.
Browne's in, all right.*

*Them Kelton midgets. Also on the make. One of
'em going for this glamour blister and runnin' 'way
back. The other one trying to box off competition for
his brother. I guess they're in—they would if they
thought they could get away with it.*

*Then there's Gates. He don't like Tony Austen. He
don't like anybody that's got more than he has, and
that's nearly everybody. People hardly ever pull a murder just for that, though.*

Quinny suddenly looked at Fane Gordon with fresh
interest.

"Look, glamour girl," he said abruptly. "A while
back you made a crack about Park Avenue gold diggers, and while you was doing it you put the eye on
this Forbes gal. How come?"

Fane Gordon seemed a little startled. She surveyed
the remains of her drink for a second, then raised the
glass and drained it.

"You don't like me, do you?" she asked, irrelevantly.

"Not a hell of a lot," admitted Quinny. "Maybe I
would have, if you had been brought up right. But
about that crack you made—"

"Park Avenue gold diggers are fairly common," she
said, with a contemptuous curl of her over-red lips.

"There are lots of them with social background, too. Like Dee Forbes."

"Yeah?" Quinny seemed deeply interested. "I've never prowled Park Avenue much. How about Dee Forbes?"

"Oh, I suppose you can't blame Dee. Her father lost his money and killed himself. A girl has to live somehow, and she doesn't know anything about making a living. Working at something, I mean."

"That all you know about her? That don't make her a gold digger, just because she ain't got any dough."

"I've heard things. Things I don't care to repeat." The girl's eyes went weary. "I'm rather sick of all this. These people and this life. There must be something else—something more exciting than staying up all night and sleeping all day, seeing the same people and hearing them say the same things—drinking, dancing, and saying no to a lot of jerks that want to marry me because I have money! Sometimes I wonder if people without money, who don't have to pretend that they have, don't have more real fun in life."

"You're comin' out of the ether, babe. Next thing you'll really start thinking. Probably hurt some at first, but just keep right on—it gets easier after a while."

Fane Gordon's hard young eyes contemplated the detective tentatively. "You're cute," she said.

Quinny recalled that she'd said that to him once before. He wasn't thrilled. "You say that to all the boys," he remarked.

"Do I? But you are different from the men I know. Why don't you take me out some time? You know all about life—you could tell me. Call me up—I'm in the book."

"Not in my book," replied the detective, firmly. "Anyhow, you don't learn about life from hearing about it. You got to do it. Right now I'm busy on the other end, with a dead man to think about." He got up. "Be seein' you, though."

He sauntered off toward the bar, looking around for Dee Forbes, but he noticed the Kelton brothers seated in the booth next the one Fane Gordon was in. From their expressions Quinny formed the idea that they had been ordered by Pierson to stay there. He grinned affably and came to a stop.

"Seen anything of the Forbes gal in the last few minutes?" he asked.

The boys looked at him sourly. Then at each other.

"She was out on that back porch where you found us," said Dave. "She sneaked out ahead of me—that's where we got the idea we could get away. I don't know whether she got out or not, but I don't remember seeing her since."

Quinny, however, recalled that the girl had been in the kitchen when they came back up. What, he wondered, had she gone down those back stairs for—and how had she returned without their seeing her, if she had gone out before the Keltons did? He couldn't answer this until he located her.

He turned his back on the booth and gave the dining-room an optical going over. Sherry Gates, he noticed, was leaning casually against the booth, apparently doing some heavy thinking, although his eyes were turned toward Inspector Pierson at the bar. Dee Forbes was nowhere in sight.

Chinese Red came slowly across the dining-room from the direction of the foyer. She had remained with

Quong Chee when Quinny returned to the main floor and apparently had just come from the offices. The detective left the booth to intercept her.

"Look," he said. "Have you seen that Dee Forbes dame—lately?"

"A little while before we went down the back stairs," replied Chinese Red. "She seemed interested in one of the dragons by the stairs."

"Yeah?" Quinny looked toward the stairway and remembered that Browne and Gates had also seemed to be interested in something in that vicinity.

"She passed the dragon on this side several times, looking around as though to see if anyone was watching her. Then she put her hand into the dragon's mouth, took it out again, and went over to the booth the·Kelton boys are sitting in now. But she wasn't there when we went to the kitchen to see the dumbwaiter."

Quinny pursed his lips and wrinkled his brow in concentration. There seemed to be a lot going on that he hadn't any idea of what it was about. Everyone in Tony Austen's party seemed to have something on his or her mind. With the exception of Fane Gordon. All she wanted was to go home.

"Did I hear you say you were looking for Miss Forbes?"

Quinny jerked his head around and saw that Sherry Gates had joined them. He replied that he was very much interested in Dee Forbes's whereabouts.

Gates shifted his gaze toward the passage under the mezzanine stairs used by waiters to reach that part of the dining-room beyond the dance floor.

"She went into that passage about five minutes or so

ago. She hasn't come out again—from this end, anyway," said the newspaper man. "Of course, she may
have left at its other end without my seeing her."

"Don't cost anything to find out if she's still there,"
said Quinny, starting toward the passage with both
Gates and Chinese Red tagging along behind him. Inspector Pierson, catching sight of the little parade moving purposefully toward the passage, decided that the
detective was up to something. He followed them, with
the determination that his ex-ace detective wasn't going
to put anything over on him.

This passage was some twenty feet long, continuing
on behind the orchestra stand and, with Chinese econ-
omy, lighted by a single light bulb in a fixture on the
wall.

Dee Forbes was lying in a crumpled heap on the
floor of the passage. For a moment both Quinny and
Chinese Red stood motionless, the latter in shocked
horror. The detective's hand passed over his forehead
and continued upward in a habitual gesture to thrust
back the derby. He frowned and leaned over the inert
heap at his feet. The tips of the girl's black pumps
gleamed with an iridescence that was no part of their
design.

"What's going on here?" Pierson's deep voice rumbled from the entrance to the passage.

"Nothing," answered Quinny. "It's already went on."

He kneeled on the floor and examined Dee Forbes.
She wasn't dead, her struggling efforts to breathe and
deep welts on her throat indicating that she had been
choked into unconsciousness.

"Dead?" demanded Pierson, joining him on the
floor.

"No," returned the detective. Something bright in the folds of her dress caught his eye. He picked it up and handed it to the inspector. "Jeez, look at this!"

The object was Tony Austen's arm band—open and empty.

Pierson stood up to examine the trinket closer to the light, with a downward glance at Dee Forbes. She was showing signs of returning consciousness.

"She got the dough out of it," said Pierson. "And then somebody took it off of her."

"Maybe." Quinny could wait for Dee Forbes's account of what had happened. Thrusting his arm under her shoulders, he raised her so that her head fell back, and rubbed her bruised throat gently with the fingers of his other hand. Her eyelids fluttered, and she moaned. "All right, sister, you're doing fine," he said. She opened her eyes wide and stared at him, shifted her gaze to the two others, and then relaxed.

"He tried to kill me!" she exclaimed huskily.

"Who did?" asked Quinny eagerly.

She shook her head in a painful negation. "I don't know—I didn't see—"

"Damn!" snorted Pierson. It wasn't sympathy.

"Where did you find that gold band?" asked the detective.

"The dragon's mouth." She closed her eyes tightly for a moment, then opened them again. "I saw—the Chinese put something in there—"

"Quong Chee?" demanded Pierson.

"Yes. I wondered what it was—then when I had a chance I put my hand in the dragon's mouth and found the band."

"With ten grand in it?" asked Pierson.

"It was open and empty," she answered. "I brought it in here to look at it. Then someone attacked me from behind."

"The Chinese, of course," growled Pierson. "If he was the one you saw drop the thing into the dragon."

"You're one of them lightning adders," observed Quinny. "You oughta get a box and a vacant lot, Chief. I never saw anyone that can add up like you can. She didn't say she saw Quong Chee put the bangle in the dragon's mouth. She said he put *something* in there. I'm betting that thing is a regular grab box—anybody that's got something to throw away will dump it in a thing like that."

"Then why was she attacked, Hite?"

"Yeah—why? If whoever put it in there knew it was empty, why bother choking somebody half to death to get it back? Maybe the thing was put in there with the dough in it. Somebody else finds it and takes the money out. First guy don't know this, but sees the girl friend here making off with it and gives her the works in this passage to get the dough back." Quinny paused briefly, then went on: "I'm laying good odds that ain't the right answer, either."

"Sounds all right," commented the inspector, frowning in contemplation of the idea.

Quinny grinned sourly. "That's what's the matter with it. Too simple. There's another answer: The murderer snitched the dough out of the band, chucked the thing away in the dragon's mouth—and then somebody saw Dee Forbes pick it out. This other somebody figures the wad is still in it, follows Forbes, and takes it away from her—all for nothing." He looked at the inspector as though expecting comment, but as his ex-chief made none, he concluded: "The one way it's less likely to be is the way you put it together."

"You sound like one of those riddle books, Hite!"

"I feel like I've been reading one. You can also take Miss Forbes's word for it that the band was empty, or you can believe she hid the money before the guy caught up and choked her."

"Thanks!" snorted Pierson, nevertheless realizing that the detective had summed up things pretty well. "Let's see what else is in that animal."

Instructing one of his men to go upstairs and bring Quong Chee to the scene, he went to the foot of the stairs. Quinny helped the Forbes girl to the nearest available chair, then followed Pierson. By that time the inspector had made quite a haul from the dragon's cavernous mouth: several empty cigarette containers, no end of used-up match books and some uninteresting if smelly cigar butts. Nothing pertinent to his quest, however. Abandoning the unsatisfied search, he strode to the chair where Quinny had deposited Dee Forbes.

"See here, my girl," he began. "It looks to me like you know more about this murder than you have admitted. How, for instance, did you know about that gold band?"

Dee Forbes returned his gaze sullenly and answered that Austen's idiosyncrasy was well known among her set.

Inspector Pierson glowered at her a moment. "I should lock you up for attempted robbery," he said. This would have been a rather wide interpretation of the criminal statutes, but not too wide for the inspector, if it served his purpose.

"I had a right to that money, if I could get it!" exclaimed the harried girl.

"Yeah?" Quinny was interested. He dropped into the chair opposite, leaned on his elbows, and directed his curious eyes at the girl. "How come you figure you rate this dough?"

"Tony Austen let me down—he did worse than that!" Dee Forbes's strained voice indicated approaching storm, her blue eyes beginning to dampen with tears. "Last summer we were engaged—Father and I were desperately poor, and what little money there was had been spent in a campaign to get me a suitable husband—"

"A husband with suitable dough," amended Quinny. "Go on."

"Tony suggested an elopement." The girl glanced around to see if any of her pals were within hearing distance. "I don't want this to go any further, please, but you'll understand better how I feel when I've told you. I agreed to go away with Tony and one afternoon last summer we went over into Jersey to get married We found a justice that was agreeable to a bribe—and we were married. The next day we returned to New York."

"So Austen is your husband?" queried Pierson, raising his shaggy eyebrows. "That *is* interesting."

"He is not!" snapped Dee. "After we returned, he said we had better not announce the marriage until he had opportunity to look up its legality. He kept me dangling for weeks, then told me one day that the marriage was not valid. Just like that!"

"That was a dirty trick," commented Quinny, reflecting that this business of getting married was a lot more complicated than he had ever supposed. "But that wouldn't keep you from having another go at it—you and Austen."

"I know." Dee Forbes's bitterness welled up in full force. "He had an answer for that, too—claimed that his last divorce had a flaw in it and he was afraid he would be risking a bigamy charge. He offered me a settlement."

"A settlement would have been lots better'n being married to a heel like that." Quinny's opinion was that Dee Forbes would have been an utter goof to turn down such an offer.

The girl made a sound of contempt. "That would have been all right with me," she said. "But he didn't even make good on that. And my Dad—"

"We know about that," interrupted the detective, understandingly. "Well, I wouldn't blame you if you had grabbed off this arm-band dough. It looks like you had a steady spot back of the old eight ball." He wanted very badly to question the girl about her unauthorized excursion down the back porches, but decided to hold it for the moment. Just as well not to add anything more to the inspector's worries.

"I'll have to take you over to Center Street and have a matron search you," said Pierson, with no trace of apology in his voice. "You could still have that money on you."

"Why don't *you* search me, if you think I have it?" the girl demanded. "I'll stand for it. I want to go home!"

Pierson shrugged. "Not my job," he said. "You'll have to go to Center Street for that."

The delegation which had been sent to bring Quong Chee from his office arrived, with their quarry between two outsized detectives.

"Here he is, Chief," said one of them, thrusting the Chinese forward roughly.

Pierson straightened up.

"What did you hide in that dragon's mouth?" he demanded. "And don't say you didn't, either. You were seen doing it."

The Chinese stared at the inspector blankly. "No can do—no can ingriss," he said.

Then the inspector really exploded. "What!" he roared. "You, too? Now *you* can't speak English—"

Quinny eyed the disturbed newcomer critically. "Funny how all these Chinese look alike," he said. "But, Inspector, this one ain't Quong Chee."

Pierson turned a wrathful eye toward the detectives. "I told you to bring Quong Chee down here—not just any Chinese you found walking around!"

"Hell, Chief," expostulated the detective. "This is the only one up there. He's been sittin' in the office ever since you left."

"I left Quong Chee up there—not this fellow! He's got away from you somehow. Madden! Dikes!" The lieutenant and another detective hurried over. "Give this place a combing—the owner, Quong Chee, has made a getaway! Listen to me, you lugs—if anyone has left this place without my permission, there is going to be hell to pay. That goes for you, too, Madden. I told you to get rid of the customers we weren't interested in. Not the suspects."

Chapter Thirteen

A RED DOOR FOR LUCK

QUITE A NUMBER of assorted Chinese were rounded up by Pierson's staff in the next few minutes, but the object of the search was elusive. The inspector had them all herded into the large kitchen for inspection (he'd given over the folly of questioning them for the time being, as he couldn't get an interpreter from headquarters before morning). Quinny believed he had never seen quite such a collection of Orientals. There were a couple of large ones—large for Chinese, that is—a fat one, two or three slim waiters, and even one hunchback. The detective couldn't remember ever having seen a Chinese hunchback before.

It was easy enough to see how Quong Chee had managed his escape from the office, but where he'd gone to was something else. The big detective who had been stationed in the office admitted that he had been watching the scene below through the window when the waiter brought tea to his employer. A short exchange of Chinese words, and then the waiter had simply sat down in Quong Chee's chair while the latter picked up the tray and walked out. The detective had turned around only to see what he supposed was the waiter leaving. They were approximately of the same build, and the substitution had passed unnoticed.

Pierson's efforts to extract any information from the restaurant staff weren't very fruitful. Apparently Quong Chee was a complete stranger to them.

"He asked me if you were going to lock him up," Quinny recalled. "I told him you probably would—and he didn't seem to like the idea much."

"Fine time to be telling me!" snapped Pierson.

"He likely has been reading pieces in the paper about mugs getting worked on with a hose and all that stuff. Scared him. Of course," Quinny added deprecatingly, "nothing like that ever happens."

"I'd like to work on somebody with a hose right now!"

Quinny wagged his head. "Do you good, too. Get rid of some of the steam that's risin' off of you. There's so much of it you lose sight of the main event—finding out who killed Tony Austen."

"There's no question of that—now."

"There ain't?" Quinny eyed Pierson speculatively. "You wouldn't go to the grand jury for an indictment against Quong Chee, just on account of him running away, would you?"

"There are other things, and there'll be more, once I get him rounded up." Pierson didn't appear particularly enthusiastic, however. He knew better than most that prosecutors, juries, and such tend to be fussy about evidence.

"What are you going to do now?" pursued the detective. "Go home, put on your slippers, and wait till your dragnet pulls in the Chinese?"

"We know everything that's happened here," said Pierson. "I'm going to clear the building, put a man on the door downstairs and maybe two or three more others around the place. Tomorrow I'll come down and see if I've missed anything. Can't do anything more until Quong Chee is brought in."

"One thing you've missed so far is how Quong Chee got the body downstairs," commented Quinny. "You won't be sure of anything till you know that."

Pierson waved a contemptuous hand. "Not important," he said. "All I want to know is who killed him—not what he did afterward."

Quinny shrugged his eyebrows. "Do it your way, Chief. I got different ideas—and I want to work on 'em. Will you tell your men to let me in and out of here and not to bother me?"

"What for?"

"I still want to know how this killing was done," explained the detective. "I have a hunch I can't join things together right until I know that. You're going to be surprised if what I got in mind comes out the way I expect it to."

"I'll be surprised all right." Pierson removed his hat and rubbed his iron-gray hair. "Now don't tell me I've been surprised before. I know it. But this case is different."

"They all are. Anyhow, do I get the pass through the lines?"

Pierson grunted. "Sure, I'll leave orders. If you get anything, though, I want to hear about it from you—not by reading the *Observer*."

Quinny thanked him, adding that he *always* had given the inspector the tip-off before he issued any news releases. This wasn't strictly true. It wasn't true at all, but the detective felt he'd always managed these things for the best interests of all concerned—and especially the welfare of Quinny Hite. He started off toward the foyer, then, seeing Chinese Red sitting dejectedly at a table near the dance floor, altered his course. She was quite alone.

"Look," said the detective softly. "Do you know what became of Quong Chee?"

The girl had watched his approach, and now her eyes seemed to chill. "I don't," she replied. "Nor would I tell you if I did."

Quinny nodded. "That's right—the last part. I mean, if you do *know*, and you do, keep it under your hair till I tell you different."

"Why do you say that I know where he is?"

"Because he ain't more than fifty feet away from you right now," stated Quinny flatly. "He can fool all the rest of us, but not you. And he hasn't left the building."

The girl's eyes were deeply troubled. She seemed trying to read the detective's thoughts as she stared up at him. "I don't know whether to trust you or not," she said.

Quinny grinned good-naturedly. "Don't matter," he said. "Just do like I say. That's probably what you'll have to do anyway. You go up to the apartment and stay with Mrs. Chee till you hear from me. I'll be back after a while, when they get the place cleared out."

Chinese Red's full lips exhibited a faint smile. "You mean Mrs. Quong. In Chinese, the last comes first."

"It does? I wish horses I bet on would do that. They start last and stay there." The detective paused, probably running through his mental scratch sheet to see if any of the entries had Chinese names. "Well, anyway, I'll get in touch with you. Don't worry too much about the old gent, either—just enough to keep in form. Dames always worry some."

The Austen party had been rounded up in the foyer as Quinny reached it. They would be escorted down in the elevator by Pierson's aids, their chief's instructions being that no outsiders be left in the restaurant or basement. The second and third floors, occupied by Chinese having no apparent connection with the murder, would of course remain accessible to the tenants, but under close surveillance by the police stationed at the building entrance. This guard would be there at all hours of the day and night until the crime had been solved. Meanwhile the restaurant would not be operated.

Quinny arrived on the sidewalk before the exodus from upstairs began. For one reason, he wanted to do a little checking on his own of who came from the restaurant. He found a disconsolate Hix standing at the curb, flanked by a number of newspapermen and photographers. On the sidewalk across the narrow, winding street was another large group, mostly Chinese, staring with absorbed interest through the fine mist at the scene. Quinny joined Hix.

"Nice mess you made out o' my joint!" Hix greeted.

"*I* made!" Quinny hoisted his eyebrows as though aggrieved. "What did I have to do with it?"

"You went and found a corpse in it." Honey Joe's tone indicated a conviction that somehow the detective had arranged for the discovery. "Put the place on the bum. Now I gotta start all over again. It was a honey, too—my joint."

"Aw, nuts, Joe, this ain't going to hurt you any," demurred Quinny. "Prob'bly be a help."

"Help, hell!" growled Hix. "Not unless I can sue the Austen guy for damages resultin' from him getting himself murdered on my property. Do you suppose maybe I could?" His expression lightened a bit.

"Sure, you can. You can sue anybody, any time, for

anything. It's collecting that's the good trick." Quinny's expression was reminiscent. "I've been sued plenty, but so far nobody ever got anything off of me that way."

Headed by Mayo Browne, looking very important, the Austen party came from Chungking Garden onto the narrow sidewalk. Flash bulbs exploded to record their exit for the edification of millions and millions of readers. One more enterprising photographer, subscribing to the conventions of his craft, did his level best to persuade Fane Gordon to sit glamorously on a fire plug. Whether or not the girl considered this a feat beyond her prowess, she declined—omitting thanks. The party hurried away toward Chatham Square for cabs.

Dee Forbes, white-faced and shaken, appeared, under escort of plain-clothes men who hadn't the least aversion to being photographed. They paused briefly, assuming expressions of grim determination and devotion to duty as the bulbs flared. In fact, they were so intent on their own advantageous showing that they let the girl shield herself behind them, to the freely expressed wrath of the lens hounds, who yelped for a retake—and got it. Only when the photographers were satisfied was Dee Forbes taken to a squad car for the trip to Police Headquarters to be subjected to the indignity of a thorough search of her person for the missing money.

Sherry Gates lounged out of the entrance, receiving a salvo of greeting from his fellow newsmen, who saw in him a chance to get the details they didn't have. Gates was superiorly affable, but definitely not giving. He was in the business himself—and for himself. He brushed away his competitors and went to the curb to give Dee Forbes a hand getting into the squad car, ignoring the hard looks bent on him by the detectives. Quinny saw Gates's eyes flick to his left—toward Pell Street—as the columnist leaned over and spoke to the girl. She nodded, and the car plunged away up the narrow, curving street.

Ten or twelve employees of Chungking Garden appeared in the doorway, including the Chinese hunchback Quinny had noticed in the kitchen. Most of them crossed the street to join others of their countrymen who were interested bystanders. Others disappeared into the muggy night. The hunchback was one of these, walking away at the side of the man the detective identified as the bartender. There was something odd about the hunchback—most of them, Quinny had noticed, carry their heads very erect. This fellow, however, walked with his bowed, his eyes on the sidewalk.

Rudely interrupting Honey Joe's lamentations with a sharp exclamation, Quinny dashed after the bartender and his misshapen companion. He caught up just as they were reaching the corner of Pell Street, turning to the left toward Mott, and trailed along after them. For a white man unobtrusively to shadow a Chinese in Chinatown is a difficult matter. The detective made no attempt to be furtive about it, but just followed along.

Reaching the intersection of Mott Street, the hunchback and his companion turned to the right, past the grocery on the corner. These Chinese groceries are more curious than appetizing to Occidental eyes. A shockingly naked and well-cooked pig crouching in the window seemed to eye Quinny with a morose expression as he scuttled by.

A short way beyond the grocery the two Chinese

turned into a hallway, dimly lighted by a single small-caliber incandescent. Once they got out of sight the detective knew they would probably be gone forever so far as he was concerned. He rushed into the hallway after them.

"Hey—wait a minute!" he shouted.

The bartender halted, turning to see who it was. The hunchback accelerated his pace toward a stairway. Quinny brushed past the bartender and seized the hunchback by the arm.

"What is this for?" demanded the infuriated Chinese.

Quinny grinned.

"Hell, what are you kicking about, Mr. Quong?" he asked. "I let you make a getaway from the restaurant, didn't I?"

With a quick movement, the detective thrust his hand up under the back of the hunchback's coat and withdrew it, bringing forth a plucked and very dead chicken. He laughed, and even the Chinese relaxed somewhat.

"That was a slick one," commented the detective. "But why a chicken?"

"In moments of need, one makes use of the material at hand," returned Quong Chee, with a wry smile.

"Why were you running away?"

"Because I could never endure being locked in a cell or even a room," replied Quong Chee. "I suffer from a disorder called claustrophobia—a horror of enclosed places."

This was a new one on Quinny. "The jug is full of people with that disease," he commented. "Only they call it the jail-house willies."

"You will not force me to return?"

Quinny shook his head. "That wasn't my idea. All I wanted was to know where you were going to be. I'll have this thing cracked in another twenty-four hours, I think."

Quong Chee stared for a reflective moment at a neon light advertising the Chinese Rathskeller across Mott Street. Then his small black eyes turned to the detective.

"It will be worth a great deal of money to me, Mr. Hite, if you can do as you say. My restaurant is closed, I am deprived of the society of my wife, and I am not fond of the notoriety that will follow. For the present, I will remain in the rooms of my friend here—Yuen Gat. I shall continue to be deformed, but with other means than the chicken."

"Which can still be eaten," amended Yuen Gat, practically.

Quinny examined the hen which he held by its limp neck, prodding it tentatively with a stubby forefinger.

"Looks like it might be a good one, too," he said. He handed it to Yuen Gat. "Okay. I think you'll be pretty safe, but don't mistake—Chinatown will be gone over with a fine-tooth comb—come daylight. Pierson's got you taped for the murder now for sure, on account of you taking it on the lam."

"We shall use caution."

"Use a lot of it. How am I going to find you, if I need you?" The detective peered up the gloomy stairs. There would be a labyrinth of small rooms up there, he knew, having visited similar buildings in this district when on the force.

"The door to Yuen Gat's room is painted the color

red, in the belief this will bring him good fortune. I trust it may have that effect on my own."

"That's fine. Keep inside the room and maybe it will."

Quinny turned and walked out into Mott Street. He retraced his trail back to Chungking Garden, but evidently now in no hurry. Sidewalk traffic had dwindled away, although through the windows of the stores he passed Quinny could see the motionless groups of Orientals standing about. The rain had slackened to a fine drizzle, and the air was heavy with the strange scents of Chinatown, disturbed by the weird cacophony of distant Chinese music.

The sights and sounds and scents of the quarter at the moment made no apparent impression on Quinny Hite. Nevertheless, his was the type of mind which absorbs a great deal subconsciously, to be brought to the surface when needed. Inspector Pierson's formula was to try to solve a puzzle with whatever evidence he had in hand, and quickly, while the detective was inclined to use the information he had as nothing more than a base to work on. It was never sufficient for him to be reasonably sure of the suspect's guilt until he was able to state with assurance just what had occurred. Motivation, a key point to the inspector, meant little to Quinny. All murders have motive, and from long experience he had concluded this ranged from slight to great —depending entirely on the murderer's mentality.

As he was about to pass a small and inelegant chop suey place near the corner of Doyers Street and Pell, he caught sight of Sherry Gates huddled over a pot of tea, his back to the windows. After a moment's hesitation, he pushed through the swinging doors and went in, stopping at the table where the newspaper man brooded over his teacup.

"Hiya, Gates!" Quinny greeted. "You're the first newspaper mug I ever saw goin' for tea."

Gates looked up, but quite without shame at having thus been caught. "I like tea," he said.

"Maybe you like it well enough to live around here some place," suggested the detective. He was fishing, but with no great hope of landing even a minnow. This man he recognized as a cagey specimen.

The newspaper man pointed out that tea may be had practically universally, to which thought Quinny concurred. Gates eyed him with frank suspicion.

"You're wondering what I'm hanging around Chinatown for," he said bluntly. "The answer is that I work on a newspaper. I'm waiting for something to break on the Austen murder."

"I thought you just wrote a column."

"A newspaper man covers anything he comes across."

"Okay—I was just asking." With a sort of salute, the detective left the restaurant. But once beyond the sight of anyone inside the place, he backed into an unlighted doorway in the next building.

That lug, he soliloquized, *is waiting for somebody— and it's a hell of a lot easier to figure out who than why. Just the same, though, I'm betting I know why, too.*

He wasn't kept waiting long. Presently a taxicab rolled into the street and drew up at the curb before the restaurant. Dee Forbes got out and hurried into the dingy resort, with a swift look up and down the street that missed Quinny completely.

For the moment, that was all the detective wanted to

know. He left the sheltered doorway and turned into Doyers Street to return to Chungking Garden. He found the bull-necked cop, Moriarity, on duty at the entrance. The place had been well evacuated by this time, although there were still a number of people standing about on the sidewalks, staring at the ancient façade with morbid interest. Honey Joe Hix hadn't moved from his post, leaning against the wall at the side of his padlocked vice emporium, ·hands thrust deeply into trousers pockets and the woe of the universe expressed in his florid countenance.

Moriarity admitted the detective without question (somewhat to Quinny's relief—he hadn't been too sure Pierson had left instructions) and he padded down the stairs to the basement. Near the elevator entrance he found another cop, who straightened up and took a belligerent step toward the detective as he emerged from the stairs.

"Okay—I'm Quin Hite!" greeted the detective, hoping the man would be properly impressed.

"Okay," repeated the officer, retreating by one step. The name meant nothing whatever to him, but he decided that this must be just one more of Pierson's homicide outfit and thus not to be interfered with by a mere uniformed cop.

Quinny walked into the hall leading to the Joss House, studying the wooden floor as he went along as though in deep concentration. Certainly there was nothing visible on the worn and discolored boards to hold his attention. The Joss House was deserted and dark, save for the luminous statue of *Chang-o*. The statue was mounted on a base consisting of three superimposed platforms of black-painted wood, forming a pyramid. The detective walked around this support, bent over for close examination. He found what he was looking for. It was impossible to step on a black-painted surface in street shoes without leaving telltale marks. On this was the unmistakable outline of a small and pointed shoe.

Impossible, that is, without precautions. Whisking a large handkerchief from his pocket and spreading it on the wood at the side of the footprints he had discovered, Quinny stepped up. This brought him close to the statue.

"Old girl, if I ain't wrong, you're holding something out on us," he murmured. He wrinkled his nose. The damned thing had an awful odor, at this range penetrating that of the smoldering joss sticks at its feet.

The statue was of wood, and *Chang-o's* voluminous robes had been elaborately carved into many folds, her arms crossed with the palms of her long hands turned up. *Not very comfortable,* he thought. Standing on the handkerchief, he poked around in the folds of *Chang-o's* garments as though searching for something. His arm brushed against one of the hands and it moved slightly. Instantly curious, he examined it more closely and discovered that not only was the hand loose, but that it could be readily detached. A hole had been bored in the arm when the statue was constructed to receive the carved hand, and in this Quinny found a rolled up handkerchief.

Getting back down from the dais, he unrolled the linen handkerchief. It was quite a large one, with the letters "AA" embroidered in a corner, and in its fold he found a small oiled-silk envelope. In this were ten one-thousand-dollar bills, crisply folded, and the odd-shaped key to the gold arm band.

Quinny raised his eyes to the imperturbably staring goddess and lifted his hat.

"What a dame!" he exclaimed softly.

Chapter Fourteen

MOTT STREET SANCTUARY

QUIN HITE wasn't at all surprised at his discovery. In fact, he would have been somewhat disappointed if he had not found the money, although it was a long shot he played on a hunch and a chance remark that the statue was the repository of the missing money. He had been quite sure it was concealed somewhere about the building, although not necessarily in the basement. No murderer with any sort of intelligence at all would carry hot money like this around while the investigation was going on.

The Joss House offered several advantages as a place to conceal the money, he reflected. The best reason was that it was easy of access, either from the street by way of the building entrance or through Hix's synthetic dive, with the additional attraction of usually being deserted. His first thought was that this person who cached Austen's bankroll here was someone that was well acquainted with Chungking Garden building, but after some study decided that it didn't necessarily follow. The folds in *Chang-o's* carved costume would offer the same suggestion to one looking for a place to hide the booty as it had to the detective, and the discovery of the loose hand could occur just as it had to him.

With the satisfying thought that whoever had put the money in the statue's arm was due for a disappointment when a return visit was made to get it out again,

Quinny stuffed his find in an inside pocket and left the Joss House to the watchful care of the moon deity.

The one source of illumination in the hall outside the Joss House was overhead, controlled by a long string. Quinny pulled the cord and plunged the corridor into darkness. Leaning against a wall, he stared at the floor for a while, and then as his eyes became adjusted to the gloom he saw a row of spots along the hall floor, very much like the ones he'd seen on the porch when he had encountered the Kelton brothers in their ill-starred attempt to leave Chungking Garden. He jerked the cord to restore illumination, then went on to the rear door, which opened into the back area.

This was a small, triangular-shaped plot, containing a number of discarded packing-cases and other refuse, for the most part neatly stacked up. This back area was on a level with the basement floor, but a brief investigation revealed that the door the detective had just come through provided the only possible entrance. The detective trudged up the stairs to the porches, pausing to examine the spots on the floor he had noticed earlier.

As he reached the door into the kitchen hallway, he stopped again, not because of anything he saw, but because of a fresh idea which popped into his mind. He stood there for a couple of minutes contemplating it. On his right sleeve there was a trace of the same phosphorescent glow as the spots on the floor.

Whoever stashed the dough in the statue probably got some of that phosphorus stuff on him, too, he thought, like I got on my sleeve. But that don't answer for the spots on the floor. If they came off shoes, how'd the stuff get on 'em. Unless he was a midget he wouldn't have to climb up on the statue. The only footprint I saw looked like a woman's, but even an ordinary-sized dame could reach the arm. Besides, you couldn't climb up on the statue—there ain't nothing to stand on. The Forbes gal's slippers looked like they mighta picked up some of the stuff, but it was only on the toes—as if she'd stood close to the thing. Anyway, nobody would pick up enough of the stuff from the statue to leave tracks where they walked.

Quinny stood a moment longer, his brow furrowed, and then his expression abruptly cleared. He nodded with satisfaction and twisted the doorknob.

"Uh-huh," he murmured as he opened the door. "That's it. I forgot about the back room!"

He ran smack into a large, strange, and startled cop as he came out of the hallway into the dining-room. Moreover, this was a member of the finest who patently did not like being startled. Not while he was illicitly helping himself to a slug from a bottle on the bar, which had been newly opened and was half emptied. The seal lay on the bar alongside the bottle.

"Who in the hell are you?" growled the cop. "Also, where in hell did you come from and where do you think you're going?"

"The name is Quinny Hite," responded the detective, not at all disturbed. "I was born on Hudson Street —quite a while ago. I heard rumors that the house was buying, so I ran all the way over." He eyed the bottle and blew out his cheeks, wiggling his eyebrows suggestively.

"Oh, Hite, eh?" The cop stared at him curiously. "I guess it's okay, then. I've heard of you—nothin' good, though."

"That just shows you ain't been going around with

the right kind of people."

"No? That's what you think, maybe. Have a drink? It's good stuff—me'n the other boys needed a little refreshments."

Quinny helped himself to a drink, standing with his back to the bar looking out at the deserted dining-room —deserted, that is, save for a couple more cops. *Funny, he thought, the police commissioner is always squawking he ain't got enough men to do a right job and Pierson leaves cops around like he can't find anything useful for 'em to do.*

A trimly suited woman just disappearing through the foyer arches caught his eye as he finished his drink, and as he reviewed the fleeting glimpse he'd had it brought a consciousness of flame-colored hair. He chided himself. Just because a dame changes from a nifty evening outfit into tailored clothes her identity shouldn't confuse a smart guy. Quinny definitely rated himself in the latter category. He set out after the girl, but without intention of catching up.

By the time he reached the foyer it was entirely unoccupied by any human being, not even by a cop, but there was the sound of hard heels clacking on the stairs leading down ultimately to the street. Quinny trailed silently along, wondering what Chinese Red was up to now, and still having a reasonable notion of where she was headed for.

I wouldn't have thought she would be sap enough to lead the cops to Quong Chee's hide-out, he thought, as he slithered along in her wake, *but I'll fade anybody that says she's going anywhere else!*

Reaching the street floor, he watched while the girl stopped for a check-out with the beefy Moriarity. He heard her say that she would return in just a little while—she needed something from the drugstore at Chatham Square. *Dames always need something from the drugstore* was the detective's thought, as he waited until she walked away from the entrance. Then he went out.

Across the street he saw a man in civilian clothes taking off after Chinese Red and recognized him as a one-time confrere named Fogarty. As soon as this other detective had got well on his job of seeing where the girl was going, Quinny applied himself to keeping Fogarty in sight, with the same object in mind. Fogarty turned left on Mott Street. So did Quinny. Chinese Red was far ahead, but visible. Mott Street, like most of the others in Chinatown, is a curving thoroughfare—the main street of the quarter.

Opposite the church at the corner of Park Street, Fogarty crossed to that side and stopped, taking up a shadowed position near the church entrance. Quinny did likewise, so far as crossing the street was concerned, but with no effort at concealment. He walked up to Fogarty.

"Where'd she go?" he asked.

Fogarty nodded to another of the innumerable eating-places of the neighborhood (there are probably more restaurants to the block in Chinatown than anywhere else in the city). "Over there," he said.

Chinese Red was plainly visible in the restaurant across the street, standing at the side of a large round table talking to one of a group of Chinese men. On the table were quite a number of dishes containing food and as she talked to the one Chinese the others kept on with their chopstick work, reaching into the various dishes to spear a succulent morsel and transferring it to their own plates. To the watching detective it seemed just plain Communism. After a short conversation, the girl left the group of diners and was lost to view through a door at the rear.

"Them Chinks sure got funny ideas about eatin'," observed Fogarty. "Notice how they swing them chopsticks inta the big bowl and come up with a piece of something and then eat it?"

"That's what we think," replied Quinny, who was beginning to regard himself as an authority on Chinese custom. "Maybe they got the same idea about us."

"Yeah-yeah!" agreed Fogarty. "I read in a book one time that they think *we're* crazy."

"Well, ain't we? You didn't have to go to the trouble readin' a book to find that out. Here we are going on midnight, staring into a chop suey joint at somebody that ain't even there."

"Where do you suppose she went to?" mused Fogarty. He was one of those cops that had risen to detective through valor, not brainwork. "Anyhow, she can't get out without us seein' her."

A tall Chinese came out of the entrance next to the restaurant. He paused in the lighted doorway and was joined by the smaller figure of a Chinese girl in the conventional black outfit worn by Chinese women—straight-lined, high-collared and with a slit in each side of the skirt at the bottom. She was pulling a raincoat about her shoulders. Both stared up into the misty darkness as though gauging the weather, and then the man raised an umbrella. They came down the couple of steps to the street and walked away.

"She can get away without *one* of us seeing her,"

said Quinny pointedly. "All I wanted to know was where she went to. Now that's off my mind, I'll leave the rest to you."

"Stick around, Hite—this is a lousy job I'm stuck with!"

"That's why I ain't stickin'. See you later."

Quinny started back up Mott Street. The Chinese couple were still in sight. One of them he had easily recognized as the black-haired Chinese girl who'd brought the liqueur to his bedside on his return to consciousness in Quong Chee's apartment. The pair walked on ahead of him on the other side of the street, crossing Pell, and beyond the grocery stopped at the entrance of the building where Quong Chee was in hiding.

Not so dumb, thought Quinny, wagging his head approvingly. *Chinese Red knew damn well she couldn't go from Chungking Garden without being tailed, so she goes to this other joint and changes to regular Chinese women-wear and the black wig. Not so dumb— but I didn't figure she was, for that matter.*

Her escort left her at the door and went on up Mott Street, while the girl faded out of sight into the hallway. Quinny followed after what he estimated was a sufficient interval for her to reach the bartender's room. The stairs were old and creaked as he mounted them, but by keeping to the side next the wall he avoided making any more than the minimum noise as he went up.

It took a good bit of prowling through the dismal, queer-smelling corridors before he located the room with the red-painted door. Voices were distinguishable, but since the conversation was in the Canton dialect, eavesdropping wasn't helpful to the detective. It wouldn't have been any more so if it had been carried on in any of the seven other Chinese dialects, for that matter. After some fretful moments, however, he heard someone speaking in English and identified the voice as Quong Chee's.

"You will arrange, then, for Ching Han to meet me at Fourteenth Street and Tenth Avenue with his car at eleven o'clock tomorrow morning. He will be prepared to drive me to the house of my friend in Boston. He will also bring a supply of money, if possible, but this is not·indispensable. I can get funds, if needful, from Ho Lan, after my arrival. At all events, I shall remain close in his house until matters have become adjusted."

"The restaurant—" This was Chinese Red.

Quong Chee interrupted.

"The restaurant will remain closed," he said. "The police will see to that, no doubt. Later, if my situation does not improve, I will arrange for my wife to join me—perhaps in San Francisco." There was a brief silence before he spoke again. "You had best return to the Garden, my child. Speak to my wife—tell her to be of good cheer. Much comes to those who wait in patience."

Sensing that the conference behind the red door was about to break up, Quinny scurried down the creaky stairs to the street. There didn't seem much point in following Chinese Red to the place where she had changed costumes, as she undoubtedly would return to Chungking Garden as soon as she had resumed the tailored outfit. Instead he walked down Pell Street to the small eating-place where he had seen Sherry Gates and Dee Forbes. They were no longer there. Speculating on the activities of this pair, he strolled back to the corner of Mott, where he leaned against a wall covered with Chinese news bulletins, which looked like oversized laundry tickets to him.

Presently he spotted Chinese Red coming toward him from the place where she'd changed clothes, and beyond, on the other side of the street, the faithful Fogarty trailing along.

"*Ho la ma,*" said Quinny, at one stroke exhausting his Chinese vocabulary. He stepped out to meet the girl.

"*Ho, fon kwa low,*" she replied, slowing up.

Quinny grinned amiably. "You got me," he said, gathering up the girl's arm and tucking it under his. "I suppose in English that means I oughta walk with you to your front gate. Okay—can do."

"You would be surprised what it means."

Quinny got an impression that he might also be shocked and didn't ask for an interpretation.

"Where's all your packages?" he asked.

"Packages?" Chinese Red seemed puzzled.

"Sure. You don't expect Moriarity to believe you spent all this time in the drugstore without buying anything, do you?"

"Oh!" The girl slackened her pace momentarily.

"You gotta pay attention to all the little details when you start out on a criminal career," Quinny cautioned.

"But I'm not!" She was indignant. "Why do you say that?"

"A little while ago I saw a little Chinese girl in Chinese clothes skittering along Mott Street with a gent with an umbrella. Looked kinda like you."

"That is absurd," denied Chinese Red, darting an

oblique and searching glance at the detective's impassive face.

"Yeah? Well, anyhow, this little girl ducked into the house next to the grocery store which has a pig in the window. You know the place?"

Chinese Red didn't answer, and they covered a few more yards of sidewalk before Quinny resumed:

"I suppose maybe she had friends in that building. Friends that live in a room with a red door." The girl uttered a half-stifled gasp. "One of 'em is thinking about taking a trip to Boston."

Chinese Red stopped and pulled her arm from under the detective's, facing him with a furious gleam in her eyes.

"You followed me!" she accused. "That was mean of you!"

"Was it you?" Quinny gave a fair imitation of a man looking surprised. "Look, beautiful, you mustn't go around doing things on your own like that. You'll only gum things up for me—and get yourself locked up as what they call an accessory after the fact."

"The police may lock me up, if they like, but Quong Chee must not be arrested. He would go crazy."

"The important thing is not to keep him out of jail, but to keep it from being permanent if he does get in," said Quinny grimly. "That's what I'm working on— and it's not going to help any for him to be going off on automobile rides. I'm going to depend on you to get word to him to stay put."

Chinese Red did not answer. They had reached the entrance to Chungking Garden, where Officer Moriarity leaned in the doorway, resentful of a post like this. He felt his talents merited more intellectual employment. He eyed Chinese Red and her escort suspiciously.

"Where's all the stuff you got at the drugstore?" he demanded.

"It's coming around on a pushcart," explained Quinny. "Fogarty's pushing it. Don't worry, Steve—the situation is well in hand."

Chinese Red looked at the detective for a moment with an expression of distrustful hope, then left him with the cop as she entered the building. The sound of her footsteps on the worn marble treads of the stairs came back to them as she ascended, then faded away.

"Where the hell did she go, Hite?" demanded Moriarity.

"*Foy yong dow,*" replied Quinny, gazing at the sign over a store across the street. "That's Chinese for 'I don't know.'"

Singularly enough, it was also the name on the sign he was looking at.

BY THE TIME Quinny Hite reached the Hotel du Nord he had finished a considerable review of what he'd learned about the murder of Tony Austen. There was to him a strong indication of the identity of the killer, but he felt there was still a lot of work to be done before he would be in a position to prove it. All too often in police work murderers have escaped punishment for lack of conclusive proof when their identity was no mystery at all.

The fusty lobby of the ancient and shabby du Nord was practically deserted when he came in. Wolfe, the night clerk, who napped whenever he had opportunity, was making full use of this chance for a bit of beneficial sleep. Quinny crossed the lobby and entered the elevator. Old Sam, the Negro operator, was sitting on a low stool reading an early edition of one of the noisier morning tabloids. He looked up at Quinny and batted his eyelids.

"Up," said the detective, wondering what was the matter with Sam's eyes.

"Yassuh," answered Sam with alacrity. He got up, closed the gate, and started the car with more zeal than he ordinarily displayed. Reaching the fourth floor, on which Quinny's room was located, Sam opened the grille and let him out. Then he sat down promptly on the stool and apparently was stricken with a bad attack of palsy.

Quinny started for his room, then changed his mind. He wondered whether Joan had really stayed on Staten Island with her aunt after the wedding fiasco of the afternoon, or had returned to the du Nord. Easy to find out. He ran up the stairs to the floor above, where the girl lived in Room 508.

Joan Fairley's room was where Quinny commonly did most of his loafing, and most of the time he had quite a lot of this to do. It was a better room than his, larger and more homelike, as theatrical hotels go. He rapped on the door panel softly, and Joan's voice inquired who it was. This was a little bit curious to Quinny, as he had what he thought was his own private rapping code ·that she always recognized. He turned the knob and opened the door. Joan was sitting forlornly on the bed.

She stared at him with eyes enlarging with something like amazed horror, not unlike the expression the detective had seen in Old Sam. Then, without uttering a sound, she closed her eyes, wavered uncertainly for a moment, and slithered to the floor in a dead faint.

Quinny was appalled. He'd never had this effect on any woman before. It was incomprehensible, that's what it was. He stepped forward, picked Joan up in his arms and deposited her on the bed, then stood there staring at her in utter bewilderment, waiting for her to snap out of it. After a minute or two, moved by his feverish curiosity about what there was in his appearance to bring about a situation like this, he went over to the bureau and inspected himself in the mirror. So far as he could see, he looked about the same as always. At least there wasn't enough change to account for Old Sam's behavior or to send girl friends into a swoon at the sight of him.

"Quinny!"

He whipped around. Joan stared at him with big eyes.

"What the hell is going on here?" he demanded. "What's the idea of passing out on me the minute I show up? And Old Sam looked like he was about to be taken with a chill when I came up. What *is* this?"

"You—" She raised her head and looked wildly around the room. Her wandering gaze came to a rest on a newspaper lying on the bureau. "There. In the paper—it said you were—*dead!*"

Quinny snorted. "Well, I ain't! Where did they ever get that crazy idea?"

He went back to the bureau and picked up the newspaper, while the girl lay back and readjusted herself to the idea that he was still among the living. On the uppermost page of the paper a reproduction of his likeness stared back at him. Underneath the picture was a story. Quinny read it with absorbed interest:

DETECTIVE HITE DROWNED IN UPPER BAY
Leaps From Ferryboat Returning From Staten Island After Wedding Upset

Late yesterday afternoon while returning from Staten Island, Quinn Hite, formerly a member of the New York police force attached to the homicide division, leaped to his death in the waters of the Upper Bay from the lower deck of the ferryboat Manhattan.

Mr. Hite had gone to New Dorp earlier in the day where he was to have married Miss Joan Farley, a night-club dancer, according to Miss Ninon Natchette, who was to have been a bridesmaid. Miss Natchette said that the bride, Miss Foley, failed to appear for the ceremony. It is believed that Mr. Hite, in a fit of depression caused by the bride's nonappearance, decided to jump from the ferryboat.

Quinn Hite, long a member of the police force, was a well-known figure in the Times Square district. At one time he was considered a valuable man on the homicide squad, but in later years had devoted his time to private work. He is said to have been partially responsible for the apprehension of Carlo Ralph, later convicted of the murders of Louis Lothrop and Desirée la Fond, and also did notable work on the Braider case last spring.

Mr. Hitt was 67 years of age and a native of New York City. At the time of his death he occupied rooms in the Hotel du Nord on Thirty-ninth Street.

AD HITE—p. 8 . . etaoin shrdlu & lr etaoin shrdlu

At a late hour last night the body of Mr. Hite had not been recovered. An effort to locate Miss Fairley has not been successful.

"It ain't so," commented Quinny, shocked and nonplussed. He laid the paper back on the bureau, then picked it up for a fresh reading.

"But Ninon—she called me at my aunt's—she said you jumped off the boat—"

"That dame is worse than the newspaper!" exploded the detective. "Neither one of 'em ever gets anything right! I *fell* off the damned boat. Look at that—67 years old! I wasn't—I ain't half that old!" Quinny struggled with some mental arithmetic, but splitting odd numbers was a problem requiring more thought than he was willing to give it.

"But Ninon didn't know—all she knew was that you—"

"They couldn't even spell my name right—there's only one 'n' in Quin, and that press agent at the Playhouse is the only guy I know that calls me 'Hitt.' Got yours wrong, too, I notice."

"—jumped overboard," continued Joan determinedly. "She said you did it for love. I was *so* thrilled!"

"They had a hell of a nerve sayin' *I* committed suicide," complained Quinny. "Especially for love. What's that 'etoine shridelu' stuff, and those letters after it?"

Joan glared at the near-bridegroom stonily. "It's Latin—means 'sucker for horses.'" It was a free translation, but fitted, she thought.

"Also, it says I was only *partly* responsible for cracking the Lothrop-la Fond case—" Quinny crumpled up the paper and threw it at, but not into, the waste basket in disgust. "Hell's bells, I could write a better story about me myself!"

"I doubt that yours would be any more accurate," returned Joan. "Perhaps you noticed that it said you 'occupied rooms in the Hotel du Nord.' Correction: Mr. Hite occupied rooms at the du Nord, one of his own and one belonging to Joan Fairley. He only used his own to sleep in."

"Yeah, maybe. Anyway, I guess I better go down and use it for some of this shut-eye stuff. I oughta look up that heel, Littlebird, first and pop him one."

"It wasn't Johnny's fault he didn't show up," said Joan. She suddenly looked worried about something. "He was here a little while ago, and awfully upset about your death."

"I bet he cried right out loud!" scoffed Quinny. "Like

a baby."

Joan gave the detective a rapid sketch of the reasons for Johnny's nonappearance at the nonmaterializing nuptials. Quinny expressed skepticism, although acknowledging the probability of the man's owing every tailor in Times Square. Joan examined her fingernails uneasily.

"You're going to be awful mad, Quinny," she said. "When I tell you this."

"What?" demanded her boy friend, apprehensively. He scented a new blow at his self-esteem.

"Johnny said he wanted something to remember you by," explained Joan. "I gave—"

"What does he want to remember me for?" interrupted Quinny. "After I see him, he's going to want to forget me—only it'll take him a while to do it. That—"

"Your radio," finished Joan. She didn't look up.

Quinny started to complete his description of Johnny Littlebird as he saw him, then paused with open mouth to stare at Joan. The radio was his only cherished possession. It was one he'd won in a raffle for the benefit of St. Somebody's Church, a short-wave set with which he'd once brought in Omaha, Nebraska.

"You gave that lug my radio!"

Joan nodded, looking a little bit scared. "I didn't know you weren't—drowned."

"Well, I'm a son of a gun!" exploded Quinny. This was laying it on pretty thick. "Me not cold in my grave yet—and that guy makes off with my short-wave set! It's—it's ghoulish, that's what it is! Now I got to go out and catch him before morning."

"Oh, don't be silly! He'll bring it back as soon as he hears that you aren't really dead."

"He will, eh? Baby, that set will be in hock by half-past eight tomorrow morning—and by nine o'clock he'll have the ticket sold for another half a buck." Quinny clamped his derby on tightly and prepared to leave. Then he thought of something else as he moved to the door. He paused, a hand on the doorknob, and glanced back at the girl. "Say, babe, how's about day after tomorrow to put on this wedding act?"

"I told you this afternoon that it is definitely, permanently off," the girl answered. There was something in the way she looked at him which gave him the uneasy feeling that she meant it. "Sorry, Quinny. I love you more than any man I've ever known—I don't know why, either—but I won't marry you. The fortune teller told me not to, the teacups say I won't, and somebody gets murdered every time we set a date. Except this time."

"This time, too." Quinny sighed. It did look that way. He related his adventures after falling overboard from the ferryboat.

"That settles it, boy friend," said Joan as he concluded. "I called my agent this afternoon after you left and told him to book me for the San Francisco job. He said I could leave tomorrow night for the Coast." She considered a moment. "I have all your money in the bank—I'll get it out and give it to you before I leave. Or would it save time if I just handed it over to your favorite bookie?"

Quinny stared at her unbelievingly for a moment, then shrugged helplessly. "Have it your own way, Jones," he said. "So far as the dough is concerned, you can keep it." On reconsideration, this seemed too broad a gesture. He hedged. "Some of it."

"Another thing, darling," the girl continued. "Anytime you want to quit this detective racket and go in for something respectable—like plumbing, or clerking in a grocery—I'll marry you. Unless I happen to meet someone on the Coast I like better."

"You might, at that," he conceded. "I mean meet somebody you liked better than me. But you're the only dame I ever saw that I could figure as Mrs. Hite. Even that redheaded Chinese girl I met downtown tonight—"

"Redheads, redheads!" exclaimed Joan. "Ever since I've known you, you've been chasing redheads! Why do you bother with me? I'm not a redhead."

"You was when I first met you," untactfully reminded Quinny. Joan, in common with her sisters of the masque, had done a little experimenting with nature, in the end deciding that the ordained color of her hair was best. "Anyhow, what I was saying was that you're the only one I ever went for—"

"For more than three days in a row, anyway. It's no good, Quinny. As long as you're a detective, I'm off of you."

"Okay, Jones. Have it your way."

Realizing that the cold metal object in his hand was the doorknob he'd been hanging onto for five minutes, he twisted it and stalked out, with an admonitory glance over his shoulder. When women get like this, there just isn't anything a guy can do about it, except give 'em time. A fine grocery clerk he'd make! A woman in love is so damned unreasonable. That made it practically all the time, since he'd noticed that women were nearly always in love with someone.

Men are different, he thought. *Love is only poisonous*

to guys in the early stages. After you get settled down comfortable to one girl, it stops bothering you. Unless, of course, some new one starts it going all over again. Now, when a dame gets love, it don't let up. Gets worse, if anything. She ain't even sure about it, either— a guy has to keep on saying he loves her long after he's quit even thinking about it.

The clock over the desk downstairs registered 2:00 a.m. when Quinny returned to the du Nord with his precious radio under his arm. There hadn't been as much difficulty in locating Johnny Littlebird as he'd expected. All you had to do was figure out where the most and best-looking girls were likely to be in Times Square at this hour of the morning. This information the detective already had before he set out.

After the radio was reinstalled in its customary place, he undressed and went to bed, lying there for some time staring vacantly at the ceiling, his hands clasped under his head and his derby pulled over to shade his eyes. Presently he stirred, reaching for the telephone and bringing it to bed with him. He called a number well known to New Yorkers—Spring 7-3100.

"Hello," he said, after an interval. "Has Inspector Pierson gone home yet? He has? Okay, is Lieutenant Madden— All right. Put him on. This is Quin Hite."

He listened for a moment, then spoke again:

. "Lieutenant? This is Hite speaking. Look—you go up to the house next to the Chinese grocery on the corner of Mott and Pell. Go up to the third floor and you'll find a door painted red. Inside you'll find the Chinese that owns Chungking Garden—Quong Chee."

He listened again, the grating sound of Madden's voice replying at some length.

"Okay—I'm telling you where he is, but don't forget to tell Pierson that I told you. On Mott near Pell. Got it? The hallway next to the grocery on the corner. All right, I'll be seeing you—one of these days."

Quinny doffed the skimmer, put out his light, and squiggled down under the bed covering.

"That'll do for tonight," he said to himself. "Tomorrow'll be something else."

Chapter Sixteen

THE SPRINGING OF QUONG CHEE

IT'S USUALLY somewhere around ten in the morning before the sun makes its appearance over the buildings lining the eastern boundary of Times Square. This belated sunrise coincides with the getting-up time of only the Square's more diligent citizenry, a far greater proportion not having seen a morning sun since adolescence—and that period most likely spent elsewhere.

Quinny Hite emerged from the Hotel du Nord on the stroke of ten-thirty—blinking in the strong sunlight which had followed the night of rain. There was much to do. He not only had this Chinatown affair to think about—and there was a lot of thinking still to be done —but he had to work out some plan to convince his beloved Jones that her place was fast at his side instead of in distant San Francisco. Well, maybe not *too* fast at his side, but within hailing distance. Previously lukewarm about this wedding business, her threatened desertion had brought him to the boiling-point. He was quite surprised to discover his own changed emotion, too.

Still, life would be kind of funny without Jones and the du Nord no longer the homey little dump it had been. Nothing would be the same.

After a swig of coffee and a brace of soggy doughnuts covered with some white stuff that looked and tasted more like talcum powder than it did sugar, the detective subwayed downtown to Prince Street and walked over to Police Headquarters. Inspector Pierson was in his office.

"Hiya, Chief?" he greeted. "Any fresh murders today?"

The official leaned back in his swivel chair and looked at Quinny with a degree more of tolerance than customary.

"Hello, Hite," he responded. He shook his head. "None so far. Thanks for the tip on Quong Chee's hide-out. We brought him in. The rest of Austen's clothes have been found, too."

Uninvited, the detective sat down in the hard wooden chair reserved for Pierson's visitors. These weren't usually very happy anyway, so it didn't make any difference whether the guest chair was comfortable or not. Quinny squirmed about in search of a better relationship between his hips and the chair surface.

"Where did you find the clothes?" he asked.

"In one of those empty boxes out in the back yard. One of the boys located them this morning."

"The back yard, eh?" Quinny pondered this over for a few silent moments, then shook his head. "That don't tell us much, I guess. Things sure did get scattered around—the body in the basement and his clothes all over the place. Did you find any of the rest of his stuff?"

"No. There wasn't anything at all in the pockets."

Quinny pushed his derby back, then reached into his pocket and brought out the handkerchief with the money and key he'd found. He laid the rolled-up handkerchief on the desk and pushed it toward the inspector.

"I found this stuff down in the Joss House after you

left last night. In the statue's arm."

Pierson unrolled the handkerchief eagerly.

"That key is the one to the gold arm band," continued the detective. "The dough in the envelope is the ten grand. First time in my life I ever packed that kind of money around with me all night."

"Very likely you never will again," said the inspector. "Last night I would have bet that Forbes woman had it concealed on her somewhere."

"Would have been a good bet, too, even if you lost," commented Quinny. "Nothing to $10,000. Nice odds. But I didn't think she had this dough on her—she didn't make enough fuss about being frisked. Look, Chief, keep this away from the papers, will you? I mean about finding the dough. I got plans."

"You think whoever put it there will come back after it," said Pierson. "I'll put some men to watch the statue."

"And gum up everything," complained Quinny bitterly. "Whoever put that dough there don't have to hurry about getting it out. They'll figure the money's safe and they can come for it any time. If you put somebody there to snoop, they'll get wise to it and just forget about it. Ten grand ain't enough to run the risk of the hot squat in Sing Sing. Besides, you think Quong Chee is your man. How's he going to get at it while you got him locked up?"

Pierson brooded over this for a few seconds. "Right!" he exclaimed. "No one will try to get anything from the statue while Quong Chee is locked up, for the simple reason that no one else knows where the money is hidden—or was."

"That's what you think," demurred Quinny. "Hell,

Chief, we don't know that the murderer put that dough there. Could have been two or three other people, and so far as we know, this murder may have more than one person back of it."

"That's one thing we can be sure of—that there were several others concerned in it," affirmed Pierson. "Quong Chee couldn't have managed it all alone."

"I still think you haven't got a case, so far as he is concerned. But, look, Chief, I'm playing ball with you —so, no snitchin' to the papers about the ten grand."

"That sounds funny, coming from you," observed Inspector Pierson, whose principal complaint on Quinny was based on the latter's propensity to dispose of news tips, at a profit. "But I'll hold it. Don't kid yourself, either, that I haven't got a case. Sure, it's not complete, but I don't need much more. The Chinese had a motive, of course, and he was on the scene at the time of the murder, and the weapon was a Chinese knife—"

"Japanese," corrected Quinny. "That's one of the things we have to find out yet—where that knife came from. It wasn't Quong Chee's—he wouldn't of had anything Jap in his place."

"No?" Pierson regarded the detective quizzically. "Maybe that's why he used it—just because smart detectives wouldn't think he had such a knife."

"That's cagey thinking, all right. But, if I was you, I'd make a try at finding out where it came from. I'm going to have a shot at it myself."

Pierson nodded uninterestedly. "Sure I will. But those things are a dime a dozen in the curio stores, I guess."

"You won't find any in a curio store, Chief," objected the detective. "That is, I don't think you will.

It's one of those suicide stickers the Japs hand down from father to son." Quinny was about to expound the knowledge he'd got from Chinese Red, when Pierson interrupted.

"Is that all you have on your mind?" The inspector yawned. Homicide has a disruptive effect on a policeman's sleep.

"No. I want you to fix it for Quong Chee to get out on bail."

Inspector Pierson instantly was wide awake again.

"Oh, you do, eh? What was your idea of turning him in, if you just wanted to have us let him go again?"

Quinny was bland. "Well, turning him in was just my duty as a citizen—"

"When did you begin to get ideas about public responsibility?" interrupted the official incredulously. Suspicion swept into his eyes as he went on: "You got something up your sleeve."

"I've always been like that." Quinny didn't explain whether he referred to public spirit or his sleeve. "I think you ought to let him out."

"You think he'll go for the money. I disagree with you. He didn't kill Austen for that. I let him go and then all we'll have to do is hunt for him from here to San Francisco. And we'd never find him."

"You won't turn him loose?"

"No!"

Quinny got up and pulled his iron hat on a little more firmly.

"Okay, Chief," he said. "I was just asking. Have you any money on you?"

"Some. Why—need a buck?"

"No. Just wonderin' if you'd take a bet that Quong

Chee is out of clink before tomorrow morning. I'm layin' five to two he's out."

Pierson declined the bet, emphatically.

"I suppose you're pulling your cops out of Chungking Garden, then," said Quinny, balancing on his heels and regarding his ex-superior tentatively.

"Sure—there's nothing more for them to do there," replied Pierson, shuffling some papers on his desk as though to impress his visitor with the idea that he would now like to be alone.

Quinny turned to leave. The inspector pulled out a lower drawer of his desk to rest his feet on and leaned back restfully.

"Well, I might as well run along," said the detective. "Be seein' you. Don't get up."

Across the street from Police Headquarters is a small building that looks as though it had been there since this part of Manhattan was farm land. Quinny mounted the worn steps to the second floor and went into an office bearing the name *Sixtus Nudel,* and under this *Attorney.* He found a dark-eyed, dark-haired young woman with skinny legs and bunioned feet sitting back of a roll-top desk in the outer office. Her name was Shirley.

"Mr. Nudel in?" demanded the detective.

"Maybe," acknowledged the girl, chomping vigorously on a wad of gum. "What do you want?"

"Mr. Nudel."

"What do you want Mr. Nudel for?"

"Tell him Quin Hite is here. I'll tell him what I want."

The ancient floor boards creaked, and an elephantine figure darkened the intersecting doorway to the outer office.

"Hello, cop," rumbled the newcomer. "Want to see me?"

" 'Lo, Six. Sure, I want to see you."

The elephant turned and strode majestically into the other room, the building shaking with his tread. It made you look around for something to hang on to when Sixtus Nudel moved about this ramshackle structure. Quinny followed him in but declined the chair the lawyer indicated.

"Won't take me a minute." Quinny was anxious to get out before the building fell in, a sensation common among Mr. Nudel's callers. "I guess you read in the papers about the Austen murder?"

"I read 'em all." Nudel's voice rolled out as though he contained a pipe organ somewhere in his vast anatomy. "All the murders, I read about. Even the ones in books. I change the names of the corpses to people I don't like. What about this Austen murder?"

"They got the restaurant owner, Quong Chee, locked up. I want you to spring him."

The lawyer wagged his head knowingly. "That's what jails are for. They build them for me to get people out of. Who pays?"

"Nobody," said Quinny, with a deprecatory lift of his hand. "You're doing this for me."

"Since when am I in the charity business?" There was a rising inflection in his voice.

"You never been in it." The detective stared at the lawyer for a second, then continued. "You ain't in it now. You're going to spring the Chinese—or—"

"Or what?" Nudel fished one of those terrible Italian cigars from a cluttered drawer and lit it.

"Remember that Rachelman stink last winter?" asked Quinny.

Sixtus Nudel remembered it too well. It had been a particularly odoriferous matter of phony bonding that had come within an ace of terminating his career—and still could, if the district attorney were able to unearth a couple of missing witnesses. "I see you remember it, all right," the detective continued. "Well, Six—I can turn up Moe Binder and Jakestein any time I want to. But I wouldn't do a thing like that, if my friend Quong Chee is sprung. You see, he don't like being in jail. You wouldn't either—even if they could find a cell with big enough doors to get you in it."

"You don't know where Binder and Jakestein are," said Nudel. His tone was calm, but his eyes were not.

"They are less than thirty minutes from here."

Quinny had no idea of telling the lawyer where these men were, even if he had known. He was sure, though, that the two East Side rats would not likely wander farther afield than could be reached in a thirty-minute journey, and that, if he had to, he could locate them in a few hours.

Nudel thought it over. "All right, 'Hite, I'll spring your man. Not on account of the mugs you speak of, though, but because I like you and might be able to ask you for a favor some time. What have they got on this fellow?"

Quinny gave the lawyer a complete account of Pierson's case—or his lack of one—against Quong Chee. The shyster wagged his huge head at the conclusion and announced that the Chinese would be free sometime during the day. Quinny took his departure.

The noon editions were out by the time he had fin-

ished his call on Nudel, and the detective bought one
to read on his way uptown. The Austen story naturally
made a couple of columns on the first page, and Quinny read the story with interest, impaired to some extent
by his failure to find any mention of himself in connection with the discovery of the crime. After a thorough search, however, he did find a six-line item announcing that Quin Hoyt, the detective believed
drowned in the Upper Bay, had been rescued by a
passing tugboat. He decided that his re-establishment
as a living entity was a matter that would call for his
personal attention. Newspapers didn't seem to be as
much interested in people who escape death as those
who didn't—and in any event they seldom got the
name right.

The old Hotel du Nord had harbored a curious assortment of guests and visitors in its time, but Quinny
found the lobby loungers in a state bordering on ex-
citement as he entered. Chinese Red was waiting for
him, and the glamorous Oriental was certainly getting
the eye from all hands present, including Hugh Bren-
ning, the manager. She was sitting calmly oblivious of
it all on one of the few really useful chairs near the
elevator, smoothly dressed in a gray tailored suit topped
with a silly little white hat—well, you just can't describe silly little white hats! Seeing the detective strid-
ing into the lobby, she arose and faced him.

"Hi!" greeted Quinny. "Been waiting long?"

"Were you expecting me?" Chinese Red seemed a
little surprised.

"Sure." He chuckled. "Matter of fact, I figured you'd
probably show up before I got out of the hay—so I got
up extra early."

"You aren't pleased to see me," observed the girl, her slant eyes narrowing. "But I can easily understand why. What you did last night was the most treacherous and mean thing I've ever heard of—" Tears seemed to glisten behind the fringe of eyelashes.

"Wait a minute!" interrupted Quinny. "That's just what you think." He looked around for something to sit on and discovered a settee in an ell off the lobby. "Come on in here—and I'll tell you about it."

The girl followed him and sat beside him on the bumpy couch, resting her slim hands on her knee.

"I never could—"

"Let me talk." Quinny put his arm restfully along the back of the settee and touched her shoulder reassuringly. "Sure, I tipped off Quong Chee's hide-out to the police. But there wasn't anything treacherous about it. Nobody told me where he was—I found out myself. But that didn't have anything to do with it, anyhow. I had a reason."

"What possible reason could there be? He trusted you."

"Not much—he didn't tell me where he was going. He'd be a sap to trust anybody he didn't know any better than he does me. Nevertheless, I just got through fixing things up now for him to get sprung—I mean for him to get out of clink."

Chinese Red stared at him with both bewildered and unbelieving eyes.

"Do you mean to say that you helped to get him arrested just to have him freed again?" she demanded.

The detective chuckled. "Does sound kinda nuts, but that's the way it is. You see, I couldn't do anything down at the restaurant with all them cops hanging around the joint. The only way I could get 'em out was to get Quong Chee in. I've got some plans that call for the restaurant carrying on as usual tonight. The cops will be pulled out—I got Pierson's word for that a while ago. Now things are in the works to get Quong Chee loose. I'm hoping Pierson won't find out about it before I get my job done, or he'll stick the cops back in."

"How are you going to get Quong Chee his freedom? He'll go crazy if they keep him locked up."

"Yeah, I know, but he'll be out before dark—don't worry."

Quinny patted her shoulder, and since it was a nice shoulder he let his hand rest there. "You wouldn't know about what it takes to get a man out of jail on a murder rap. It's, uh, complicated. Couldn't do it at all, if Pierson really had a case. Now, look, this is important. I don't know what time Quong Chee will get out —the later the better—but I want you to see that the restaurant is going full blast, same as usual, tonight. You'll do that?"

Chinese Red nodded.

"I'll see you sometime tonight—"

Quinny broke off, and a look of utter consternation spread over his face. He withdrew his hand hastily from Chinese Red's shoulder, but not anywhere near quick enough to dodge the irate glare of a girl just arriving in the hotel lobby. Life had a new complication. The girl was Joan.

Chapter Seventeen

THE BARWIN LIBRARY

QUINNY LEFT CHINESE RED sitting in the alcove and caught Joan at the elevator. Joan's plan had been to reach the elevator and escape to her room before the detective caught up with explanations of his meretricious behavior. He was singularly good at explanations. But the du Nord elevator operator spent most of his time on the upper floors, where there was less chance of extraterritorial employment being thrust upon him. Baffled, Joan turned to face the oncoming explanation.

"This ain't what you think, Jones—" Quinny began earnestly.

"It never is!" the girl retorted. She drew herself up to the proud height of five feet four—plus heels. "For that matter, I don't know what you refer to."

"You do, too. About me talking to the Chinese girl—"

"It is not of the least importance to me who—whom —you talk to. That is your own affair!" She stepped back and swept him with a gaze that she imagined was one of haughty nonchalance instead of bright anger.

"Aw, now, listen! That's Chinese Red—she's a client."

"With you, the client of today is the sweetheart of tomorrow!"

The elevator clanked to a stop at her elbow and the grille door slid open. Old Sam poked his head out. "Goin' up," he said. Joan dodged Quinny's restraining hand and got in.

"She is not!" disclaimed the detective. "You know I don't go for anybody but you."

"You may go for anyone you want to, Quinny. I'm through!"

"Goin' up?" suggested Old Sam hopefully.

"For heaven's sake, yes! Go on, Sam."

"I'm goin'."

The door clanged shut—a good bit like a cell door, Quinny thought irrelevantly. He stood for a minute, his eyes, following the ascending car, giving him the expression of someone about to swoon. He sighed and returned to Chinese Red, who was watching him curiously. So were most of the others scattered about the lobby.

"Who was that?" queried Chinese Red as he rejoined her. "Your sweetheart?"

"Well—yes and no," parried the detective. "Yesterday she was, but today it seems like she ain't. We were going to get married yesterday afternoon, but it fell through." He shrugged his shoulders helplessly. "That's the way things go sometimes. Skip it. You'd better go back downtown and see if the cops have been pulled out of the restaurant. If they're gone, get the place ready for business."

The girl arose and Quinny walked with her toward the hotel entrance.

"Another thing, too—you don't know whether Quong Chee's got a lawyer, do you?"

"He has one who attends to his business affairs. I think he will probably get in touch with him about this."

"You tell his lawyer to lay off. This takes skulduggery—and I have a mouthpiece on the job who knows how to handle it. He's already working on it." They reached the sidewalk and the detective hailed a cab. "I'll call you after a while. Right now I got some things to do uptown."

Chinese Red got into the cab, but before Quinny could close the door, she leaned forward, her eyes showing amusement.

"Say to your girl friend not to be jealous of me, that my interest in you is not for love, but something much more important."

Quinny grunted. "Joan don't think there is *anything* more important than love." He closed the door and then watched the cab, which looked like one of Turner's sunsets on wheels, as it rolled off toward Eighth Avenue. *Funny stuff, love,* he mused. *An' damned if I don't think I'm catching it!*

After a short debate whether or not to make another effort to placate Joan, he decided that a recess might do more good and headed for Times Square. He wanted to find Sherry Gates, but hadn't much idea of where to look for him at this time of day, and didn't know where he lived. Not that the latter information would have been of much use anyway—newspaper men never hang around their rooms unless they are asleep. Crossing Forty-second Street he saw Abe Katz standing in front of the Rialto Theater, looking at the photographs of a seven-reel epic called *The Gorilla's Bride.* Abe Katz made a precarious living by the collection of unsavory news items for one of the baser columnists.

"The gorilla get your girl friend?" Quinny asked, eyeing the startling exhibition in the frame. "Or was you the gorilla in this opera?"

" 'Lo, Hite," greeted Abe. "Hear you're up to your ankles in blood again."

"Not that deep," returned the detective. "Say, you know Sherry Gates, don't you?"

"Sure, I know that drip. So what?"

"Where does he hang out? This time of day, I mean."

There was little that transpired in Times Square that Abe Katz didn't know, and he knew the habits of Times Square citizenry to a degree sometimes unpleasantly surprising to the latter. Sherry Gates, it seemed, was often to be found in a small bar on Fifty-first Street.

The information from Katz was good. Quinny found Gates draped over a drink at one end of the bar, evidently working on notes for his column. He lifted his eyes and nodded to the detective, who made a show of surprise at thus encountering the columnist.

"Drink?" invited Quinny.

Gates shook his head. "Never drink in the afternoon," he said. "Just one to get myself together, and I've had that one. What are you doing in this neighborhood? Thought you were working on Austen's murder."

"That's all washed up," said the detective, regretfully. "Pierson's got the Chinaman locked up, or didn't you know?"

"It's in the afternoon sheets," replied Gates. He regarded the detective tentatively, then went on: "He's got a lousy case, though, unless he's got something I don't know about."

"He's got enough to convince him, anyway," said Quinny, indifferently. "He's pulling his cops out of

Chungking Garden. He wouldn't do that if he wasn't pretty sure."

"I suppose not." Gates didn't seem very interested, returning to his notes.

"The way I look at it, though," Quinny pursued, "he's got just as good a case against you. Especially after nailing you with the knife in your pocket."

Gates grunted disdainfully. "Not my pocket," he pointed out. "Anyhow, what would I do a thing like that for? Sure, Austen and I had a scrap, but if I murdered everyone I had a fight with I'd be pretty busy." He grinned saturninely.

"Dough—that would be your motive. You'd kill a man quick for ten thousand dollars—if you thought you could get away with it."

"Thanks. But that wouldn't be enough."

"I wonder what became of that dough, anyway? So far as I know, it's not been found." Quinny's eyes were busy inspecting a poster back of the bar.

Gates shrugged. "Austen probably didn't have it on him. Couldn't they check at his apartment? His man would know, I think."

"Oh, he had it on him, all right. What would you do with that much dough, Gates?"

"Take a week off. Shut up, will you? I've got to get some stuff together for my column." The newspaper man poised his pencil ,and screwed his eyebrows together.

"Okay. I'm going, anyway. Say, I hear your sheet— the *Examiner*—is folding."

Gates nodded. "Any day now."

Quinny dropped a quarter on the bar and prepared to leave. "Then it's WPA for you. So long."

He walked out of the bar and turned toward Sixth Avenue, but after passing a couple of stores, he retraced his steps. When he was once more in front of the small barroom, he saw that Gates had left his stool. Quinny re-entered, going on toward the back. Gates was in the telephone booth.

"—open again tonight," the detective overheard as he passed the booth. Gates glanced through the glass door, said something Quinny didn't catch, and then hung up.

"You here again?" snapped Gates as he emerged.

"Yeah. I forgot to ask you if you know this Laura Barwin, Austen's aunt."

"I know who she is, but I've not met her," replied Gates. "Thought you weren't working on the case."

"Just cleaning up a couple of details for Pierson—that's all," explained Quinny. "Do you know where she lives?"

"Probably somewhere on Park Avenue. Why don't you look in the phone book?"

Quinny took the suggestion and found Laura Barwin listed with an address on upper Fifth Avenue—somewhere in the Nineties, he judged.

"What do you know about this Barwin dame?" the detective asked as he closed the telephone book. He walked toward the front of the bar, with Gates at his side.

"Nothing much, except that she's well up in the chips, and shows up once in a while in Fifty-second Street, usually with Tony. Good-looking, too, considering her age."

"Gigolo-minded?"

Gates smiled crisply. "I think not. She isn't that type at all, from what I've seen of her. You'll get what I mean, if that's where you're headed for."

"I am," concluded Quinny.

Laura Barwin did not, as the detective supposed, live in an apartment building, but in a rare old dwelling in the upper reaches of Fifth Avenue opposite Central Park. There are not many of these left nowadays and few of those are occupied. He climbed the steps, which were flanked on each side by gargoyle-like animals, and pressed the doorbell button. After a short wait, Mrs. Barwin's housekeeper confronted him.

"I want to see Mrs. Barwin," said Quinny. He liked the looks of the pleasant-faced woman holding the door.

"Mrs. Barwin isn't seeing anyone today," the housekeeper said. "There's been—a death in the family."

"Yeah, I know," he nodded. "That's what I'm here about. I'm a detective." He didn't think it would be helpful to include the amplifying word, *private*.

"Oh!" The housekeeper viewed him with new interest. "Will you wait? I'll tell Mrs. Barwin you are here."

Quinny stood in the reception hall, glancing curiously about him. Double doors, which he thought opened into a living-room, were only a step or two from where he was standing, and he moved over to peek in. It was to him a completely amazing room. He thought he had never seen so much carved wood in his life—elaborate teakwood stands and tables, with rare porcelains scattered about like dime-store crockery.

The housekeeper returned, saying that Mrs. Barwin would see him for a few minutes. She took him into a large room at the rear of the house that was used as a library, although to the detective's eye it looked more like a museum. Chinese prints adorned the walls and a vast amount of Orientalia occupied every available nook. Quinny sat down on a red lacquered chair that failed completely to measure up to his idea of comfort. The scene reminded him that the Barwins had spent some years in the Far East. He decided that they'd brought most of the Orient back with them.

As footsteps echoed on the floor outside the room the detective stood up, partly to be polite and incidentally because he wasn't getting any rest from the chair. A tall, slender woman entered, paused, and looked toward Quinny with eyes that seemed very weary.

"Mr. Hite?" she asked.

"Yeah. You're Mrs. Barwin, I guess." The woman inclined her head slightly. "I—I'm kinda sorry to bother you like this, Mrs. Barwin, but there were a couple of things I wanted to ask you."

Mrs. Barwin sank onto a chair. "Won't you sit down?" she said. "This has been a terrible shock to me."

Quinny compromised by leaning against a heavily carved library table.

"This party Mr. Austen threw last night," he began awkwardly. "Did you know any of his guests?"

"Yes, of course. Not intimately—they were all a little young for me. The Gordon child I've known since she was a baby. Mayo Browne has been here with Tony quite often—they were great chums, you know. The Kelton boys are old acquaintances, too. The others I did not know quite so well."

The detective considered what she had said for an interval. "The Keltons—they've been here lots?"

"Occasionally. Not a great deal, though—like all

these young people, they preferred the night clubs for their social life."

"Do you know Sherry Gates?"

"The newspaper man?" Quinny nodded, and Mrs. Barwin managed a trace of a smile. "I guess almost everyone knows him. He's into everything."

"I don't suppose he ever came here, did he?" Quinny eyed the woman narrowly as he asked the question.

"To my house?" Mrs. Barwin seemed surprised. "Why, I don't know. Last season I gave some parties here, with a great many guests. He might have been present at one of these. I believe he and Tony were rather friendly at one time."

"Not lately, though," suggested Quinny. "They had a big fight a few nights ago."

"Poor Tony was, well, inclined to be belligerent at times," said the woman, sighing. "But he didn't make enemies because of his fights. He always regretted them afterward and made amends."

"Some people are like that." Quinny wagged his head understandingly. "You wouldn't know, I suppose, whether he was wearing his watch last night?"

"It just so happens that I do," said Mrs. Barwin, her eyes curious. "Tony was here just before he left to meet his party. I remember that he kept looking at it, as though he thought he was going to be late. It was the last time I saw him." Distress flooded her expression.

"Could you describe it? You see, we didn't find no watch—yet."

"It was one I gave him two years ago—a Swiss watch, with Roman numerals on the dial and the word *Chur.*" She spelled the name for the detective, otherwise he might have gone around looking for a wristwatch with *Koor* on its face. "Chur is, of course, the Swiss town where it was made."

"What sort of strap did it have?"

"Gold mesh. I should think about three quarters of an inch wide."

Quinny looked around the library.

"You have a lot of Chinese stuff, Mrs. Barwin," he said.

"Oh, but it isn't all Chinese. That is my late husband's collection from the Orient. We lived out there for several years."

"I heard that." Quinny pushed himself away from the table, taking a step toward Mrs. Barwin. "Have you got one of those hara-kiri knives the Japs use?"

"There is one in Mr. Barwin's collection." She rose to her feet and went across the room toward a glass-topped cabinet. "It is here in this— Why, it's gone!"

Quinny, following along after her, looked at the case. There were quite a number of small objects contained in it, each with a small card of descriptive matter close by.

"How long's it been since you looked in this case?"

Mrs. Barwin turned her gaze to his, a faintly puzzled light in her rather large eyes.

"I don't know, really," she said. "It may have been weeks—or even longer. And even then I probably wouldn't have noticed the knife was missing."

"That's what I was afraid of," returned Quinny. "You see, it's a pretty sure bet that your nephew was killed with that same knife."

"But—who—"

"I know who," answered the detective. "And I'm pretty near ready to prove it now."

Chapter Eighteen

THE BANTAM BAR

QUINNY HITE came into the Bantam Bar about six o'clock. The Bantam Bar was a long way removed from any of his customary hangouts, geographically, socially, and financially. Particularly the latter. The place was an adjunct of Club Flamingo, although an alliance between bantams and flamingos seems a slight distortion of ornithological science. In Fifty-second Street night spots this would be a matter of no concern —or to a Times Square detective, either.

He found Peggy Long with her feet hooked on the rungs of a high bar stool toying with a Coca-Cola in the fashion of girls who hope someone will happen along and provide a slug of stouter stuff. Her eyes brightened as they rested on Quinny, and he drew up alongside, viewing the soft drink with lofty disfavor.

"What's that?" he asked.

"Coca-Cola."

"That's what I thought," he said. "How's if I buy you a slug of rum to put in it?"

"I wouldn't tell anyone." Peggy pushed the glass toward him. "Anything new on the murder?"

"What's in the papers?" He signaled a bartender. "I ain't had a chance to look at 'em yet—I just got up."

The bartender took his order before the girl replied.

"There isn't much in the papers that I didn't know last night, except that Quong Chee has been caught and is being held. The *Observer* says Chungking Garden will reopen tonight. I thought it would be closed until this was cleared up."

"If they have somebody charged with the murder, it is cleared up—so far as the police department is concerned."

The drinks were placed on the bar in front of the detective. He picked up the glass of rum and poured it into the Coca-Cola, then stirred it briskly with a muddler before pushing the mixture toward the girl. Then he picked up his own drink.

"Ho!" he said, now having adopted the Chinese vernacular within reasonable limits. He drained the glass, shivered slightly with appreciation, and put the glass back on the bar.

Quinny was about to ask what else she had read, when the Kelton brothers sauntered in. Seeing Peggy and the detective at the bar, they came over. Quinny regarded it as a rare stroke of luck that he and the girl were already provided with drinks. These lizards could buy their own—and if they did, he thought, they most likely would be establishing a precedent.

"Hello, Peggy," greeted the older one, Dave. "What's moving?"

"I hear you and Fane Gordon were bicycling in Central Park this afternoon," she replied. "I didn't know you had a bicycle."

Dave grinned affably and leaned with his forearms on the bar. Ward Kelton stood behind him, rather stiffly. Apparently he didn't wholly approve of his brother's fraternizing with people like Peggy Long and the detective.

"I haven't," said Dave. "But Fane has. I was teaching her to ride it."

"I see." Peggy took a tentative sip of her drink. "Well, now that some of your competition is out of the way, perhaps you'll make better progress. And I don't mean on a bicycle."

Dave Kelton hoisted his eyebrows and grinned good-naturedly, but made no reply. Then he noticed that Quinny was eyeing his wrist with frank curiosity. Dave altered his position to lean on his right elbow, dropping the other arm to his side.

"Hello, detective," he greeted, as though not having noticed Quinny before. The grin faded.

"Hello," responded Quinny. "Le's see that watch you're wearing."

"What for?" Dave Kelton assumed an expression of surprise that wasn't remarkably convincing.

"I think it's Austen's."

Dave made no answer for a few seconds, then brought his left wrist back into view. "It is," he said shortly. "I found it in my pocket when I got home last night. How it got there I have no idea."

"Pixies, no doubt," Quinny sneered. "So you just found it and decided to keep it. You wouldn't figure it might look kinda funny to be caught wearing the murdered man's watch."

Dave's face flushed. "I didn't know what to do about it," he asserted. "If I left it at home, the watch might have been found by someone else."

"You expected the police might frisk your joint," suggested the detective.

"No. I simply thought it best to carry it with me until there was an opportunity to turn it over to the authorities."

"Okay. You didn't discover the watch till you got

home, you say. All the time you were down there last night you had it in your pocket, but you didn't notice it until you got home. Boloney!"

"It was not in my pocket when I left Chungking Garden—I'm sure of that. When we came out, I lit a cigarette just as we started up the street. I always carry my cigarettes in that pocket, and if the watch had been there I would have found it then."

"Was that the last cigarette you smoked before you got home?" Quinny thought the explanation weak. "Or did you finish out the evening on somebody else's cigarettes?"

"As a matter of fact, the reason I recall lighting a cigarette as we left Chinatown is because it was the last one in the package. I didn't buy a fresh pack."

This statement contained a lot more logic, the detective thought, as he considered it.

"Do you think somebody slipped the biscuit in your pocket on the way uptown? I suppose you all got in the same cab—six of you: the Gordon, Rita Camonez, Browne, your brother, and Peggy here."

"There wasn't room for me," corrected Peggy Long. "I went uptown in a cab by myself and met the others at Club Flamingo."

"Five of you came back together, then," Quinny amended, his eyes on Dave. "Who was sitting next to you?"

"Mayo Browne sat in the middle, between Rita and Fane. Ward and I sat on the folding seats," explained Dave.

"Which way did you face?"

"Forward, of course—the way those seats are arranged to be sat on."

"People don't always sit that way on them, though," observed Quinny. "All right, buddy, no one could have slipped anything in your side coat pocket from the back seat without one of the other two seeing him—or her."

"I didn't say any of them did," complained Dave Kelton. "Nor did I say I thought it had been placed in my pocket during the ride uptown. All I know is that it was there when I got home—and that was hours after we left Chungking Garden."

"Another thing you didn't say was that it couldn't have been Ward Kelton who donated the timepiece to his big brother—"

"That's a God-damned lie!" exclaimed Ward, for the first time breaking his silence. His small dark eyes shone with an anger that seemed too intense to be contained in his undersized body.

Quinny regarded him unemotionally. "Dave didn't say it couldn't have been you—"

Dave interrupted. "I didn't say it might have been, either. Of course it wasn't Ward. Why should he?"

"Don't ask me." The detective moved his shoulders in a careless gesture. "All I know is you *say* somebody loaded you up with the ticker. I'm not saying I believe that, but, if someone did, when was it planted on you? Who had the opportunity?"

"I can't answer that, naturally," snapped Dave. "Any number of people could have done it. To repeat, the first I knew of the watch was after I had reached home, when I emptied my pockets before going to bed. We were at Club Flamingo until three this morning."

"Who was?"

"Why, at first the six of us. Then Fane's aunt joined us, and later Dee Forbes came along."

"Anyone else?" persisted Quinny.

"No one *you* ever heard of—not anyone that was at Chungking Garden last night."

"How about Gates? Did you see him after the show downtown?"

Dave Kelton shook his head, but his brother broke in with the assertion that Gates had been in and out of Club Flamingo a couple of times while they were there.

"That's right. I do remember seeing Sherry sometime after our arrival at the club. He cut in on someone who was dancing with Dee Forbes and after the number brought her to our table."

"Did he sit down with you?" asked Quinny.

"No. He stood there for a couple of minutes, but no one invited him to join us, so he went away."

"None of this seems to mean a damned thing," commented the detective after a little consideration. "We get right back to the beginning, Kelton. You say you found the watch after you got home. I can't say you didn't, but you can't prove it by anybody else than him." He indicated Ward. "And he don't count--he'd back you up, no matter what you said. I don't suppose you found the ten grand in your other pocket—or in one of your shoes, or somewhere?"

"I did not."

Quinny looked sympathetic. "That's too bad. Ten thousand might have come in right handy to a couple of boys that don't know how to do anything to earn money."

"That's no joke, either," commented Dave, gloomily. "Family background isn't worth to us nearly what a good course in plumbing or something would have been."

"Well, keep your chins up," counseled Quinny. "Maybe one of you'll get to be *Mister* Fane Gordon, and ride your own bicycle. But listen, brother, you better shake yourself down to police headquarters and turn in Austen's tick-tick. Then, after Pierson gets through asking you more questions than even the Quiz Kids could answer, you make sure you keep away from Chungking Garden. I mean, don't wander over there for a dish of chow mein or something. Might upset your stomachs."

"Don't be stupid," returned Dave Kelton. "I'll take the watch down, as you suggest, but Chungking Garden is off my list. It's not open, anyway, I guess—after last night."

"Peggy read in the paper that it is—or will be. Oughta do a big business, too, with the curiosity-seekers and all."

"Who will run it while Quong Chee's locked up?" asked Ward Kelton. "The Novatoff girl?"

"I shouldn't think so—it's a corporation. They'll put some other Chinese in charge, I fancy." Dave said this with an air of knowing all about corporation procedure. "Well, come on, Ward, we might as well go down and face Pierson."

The two brothers left the Bantam Bar, and, perhaps not for the first time, with unquenched thirst. Drinking, though, seemed not to be on their minds at the moment.

"You know," Peggy suddenly burst out, "sometimes I feel sorry for those two nitwits. I believe they don't have even enough to eat sometimes, and how they manage the clothes problem is a complete mystery. You can't fly around the nighteries without being pretty well dressed."

"No, you can't," agreed Quinny, sagely. At this precise moment his wardrobe consisted of what he had on, plus fifty percent of the suit he'd almost been drowned in and the promise of another from a man now in jail on a homicide charge. He added with feeling, "You can't pick suits off them elm trees in Rockefeller Center, neither. Well, pal, I got to skitter along. Maybe I'll see you again some time."

"I'll be looking forward to it," chirped Peggy. "Thanks for the rum."

Quinny tipped his derby and went out into Fifty-second Street. *Nice bunch of hoodlums I'm going with these days,* he thought, as he stepped along briskly toward Broadway, some two or three blocks away. *Next thing, I'll be turning into one of these barroom aristocrats on the prowl for a chicken with plenty gravy so's I won't have to work. Maybe not such a dumb idea, at that, with Jones legging out on me for San Francisco!*

Quinny returned to Doyers Street about eight-thirty, to find that it had subsided into June night normalcy. A big Chinatown bus had unloaded its cargo of sightseers, who were at the moment trooping timorously into Hix's basement. The proprietor stood at the side of the steps, apparently in a rare good humor. His rolling voice floated across the street to where the detective had halted in a doorway, a voice well trained in carnival device. Lights and music from the top floor indicated that Chungking Garden was once more in operation.

Directly across the street from the detective was the small chop suey house where the night before he had seen Gates. From time to time he glanced toward its windows, which permitted a full view of the interior. There were few customers in the place, and these Chinese, with a lone white woman seated at a table toward the rear—partially screened from sidewalk observation.

For a few minutes the detective remained in his sheltering doorway, staring across at the scrubby little restaurant, then, apparently arriving at a conclusion, he crossed the street and entered. As he did so, the woman turned her head and her expression resolved from expectancy to unpleasant surprise. It was Dee Forbes.

"Hello," Quinny greeted as he stopped at her table.

The girl frowned coldly.

"What do you want?" she demanded.

Quinny eyed the food a neighboring Chinese was dexterously chopsticking into his mouth, then looked back at the girl.

"Well, that guy seems to like what *he's* got," he equivocated. His eyes hardened. "But that ain't what I'm looking for."

"Why don't you say what it is, then?"

"Thanks. I will." The detective sat down in the vacant chair on the other side of the table. "I want you to go home."

Dee Forbes stared at him with uneasy belligerence.

"What do you have to do with my movements?" she demanded.

Quinny's hand moved in a gesture of complete indifference.

"Nothing," he said. "But they're interesting—and maybe to the cops too damn' interesting. Now, look, you—"

"The police aren't interested in me!"

"They will be, if you hang around down here long enough." The detective hitched his chair a little closer to the table the better to rest his elbow. "You uptown urchins don't fit into the picture in Chinatown. Take my tip—and beat it."

"I don't know why I should!" There was a tinge of defiant fear in the girl's voice.

Quinny sighed. Women make things so difficult when you are only trying to be helpful!

"Listen, dope," he said, earnestly. "I'm a softy, see. A pushover for dames with a sad-sad story. You got that kind of stuff on you. You been getting life with the peeling took off. On account of all that I'm sorry for you—"

"You needn't be!" flared Dee.

"I can't help it—it's just the kind of sissy I am." He nodded a vigorous affirmation. Then he frowned. "Look, baby, last night you picked up Tony Austen's money bangle out of that dragon's mouth. Then you went downstairs looking for a place to stash the dough until the shooting was all over. You found that place in the statue's arm—probably the same way I did. You came back up and was going to drop the band back where you found it when somebody throttled you. You say you don't know who it was. Maybe I think you lied about that, but maybe you didn't. To me, it don't matter. What I'm telling you now is to forget that dough and go home."

"I have a right to it—if I can get it!"

"Sure, sure," granted the detective. "But you can't get it. It ain't where you left it any more."

"What makes you think I did?" Somewhat belatedly the girl realized her admissions.

"You got some of that shiny stuff off of the statue in the Joss House on your shoes when you hid the money," he said. "The Kelton lads saw you on the back stairway. What the hell? Le's me and you not argue. I'll stick you in a cab and send you back uptown." He got up.

"I can take care of myself!"

Quinny nodded. "Yeah—I know. Right now, though, I'm taking care of you. Come on."

"I won't!"

"Either you do as I say and be a nice girl, or else you'll be a bad girl and go to jail," replied the detective, indifferently. "Don't be a sap. I'm telling you the Austen dough is locked up in the safe at police headquarters, so there ain't any use of you hanging around on the chance of getting it."

Dee Forbes arose reluctantly. "Then why are you so anxious to get me out of Chinatown?"

"Because I don't want you passing the word around that the dough ain't there. I figure you've had all the trouble you can hold. But I don't have the same feeling about some other people. You've got a date with somebody here in this joint. You aren't keeping it."

Dee Forbes seemed to realize the futility of her position. Without saying anything further she started for the door, with the detective catching up before she reached it. He was stuck with her check for a pot of tea, which delayed him momentarily. On the sidewalk he loaded her into a cab and watched it until it disappeared around the corner of Pell Street.

Having disposed of the girl to his satisfaction, he turned toward Chungking Garden, a half block away. At the basement entrance he found Honey Joe Hix en-

gaged in a selling campaign directed at a small group
of tourists who didn't seem convinced that Hix's horror
depot was likely to be worth fifty cents a head. The
carnival man had doubled the admittance fee, now that
he had an authentic murder scene to display.

"The chance of a lifetime!" he was declaiming as
Quinny came up. "Only last night a man, a human being, was foully murdered—" His eyes, wandering in
true pitchman fashion, caught sight of the detective.
"And there stands the man who discovered this crime
of the century! Quin Hite—old Eagle Eye, the man
with a bloodhound's nose—"

"Nix, Joe!" objected Quinny, before Hix could get
any further with his zoological panegyric. "No use
building me up. They can see me for nothing. When's
the next rubberneck wagon due?"

"About a half hour." Honey Joe felt that Quinny's
use of the word rubberneck in the presence of suckers
was in bad taste. He scowled fleetingly.

Quinny didn't care very much for the post of outside
attraction to the opium den, either, and went on to the
building entrance just beyond the basement steps. The
same Chinese was operating the elevator. Whether or
not the boy remembered the detective was something
Quinny wasn't sure of. At least the operator displayed
no interest in him, even when asked if Quong Chee
was upstairs. He said he didn't know.

Chungking Garden was crowded. Quinny stopped in
one of the arched doorways opening into the main dining-room for a few moments, looking for either the
proprietor or Chinese Red. Neither was in sight, so he
went around under the mezzanine to the dragon-
guarded stairway. From here he could see the windows

of the Chinese owner's office, but the only occupant seemed to be a uniformed and bored-looking cop sitting at the desk. Evidently Inspector Pierson still believed these offices to be the scene of the murder, and had stationed an officer there. One lonely cop wouldn't interfere with the detective's plans, he decided.

Quinny found quite a number of diners on the mezzanine balcony as he mounted the stairs and turned toward Quong Chee's apartment. He wondered whether Chinese Red planned to start the show as usual, and thought she probably might have that intention. He pressed the bell button at the side of the door, which was presently opened by a thin-visaged Chinese, who frowned questioningly at the detective.

"Quong Chee," said Quinny. "Say Mr. Hite."

The Oriental hesitated a moment, then closed the door. The sound of his shuffling footsteps faded away and shortly after returned. The detective was admitted. He found Quong Chee in what appeared to be a small library—and also in a bad humor.

"I must thank you for a very bad night," Quong Chee greeted. "It was even more disturbing to find my faith in someone to be so badly placed."

"I know," Quinny replied. "But there wasn't no other way out. I had to get you locked up to finish my job. You needn't get upset about your faith in me, though. Just keep it flying—I'll have this thing cracked in just a little while now. Anyway, I got you out of the hoosegow, didn't I?"

"I am for the moment free, if that is what you mean," admitted the Chinese. "Which makes your actions all the more puzzling. What next?"

Chinese Red came into the room, dressed in an evening outfit similar to the one she'd worn last night. She stopped in the doorway and looked at the detective.

"Opening the show—like usual?" asked Quinny.

"Like usual," she said, smiling.

"Could you skip it?" continued the detective. "I want to borrow you. It's important."

The girl eyed him doubtfully, then glanced at Quong Chee.

"You could send word to the orchestra leader," said the Chinese. "Yee Ling will take your message."

"Very well, *fa chun*," acquiesced Chinese Red. She looked at the detective expectantly.

"Do it, then," said Quinny. "Can you get into the black-haired outfit before the show starts?"

."Yes."

"Okay. Meet me on the terrace by the big crock as soon as you can." Quinny looked at Quong Chee. "I think you better stay in the apartment tonight. Don't go out in the restaurant—unless you don't mind being pointed out as the man who killed Tony Austen by all them people. In that case, it don't make any difference."

"I shall remain here."

"I'll see you later, then—with good news, I hope."

Quinny made his way from the apartment to the terrace. Now that fine weather had returned, the terrace had a quite different aspect. Tables had been brought out for the use of the Garden's clientele whose taste ran to dinner *al fresco*, although no diners were present at the moment. Wall lamps designed as miniature pagodas supplied soft illumination. The detective crossed the terrace to the large urn, stopping to gaze out over the roof tops, but from his expression he wasn't seeing anything there.

The best chance, he was thinking, *would be when the show is on. Not so many people coming in or going out. The ones from the Chinatown bus are either up here or out of the building by this time—and there ain't likely to be another bus for a while. Hix's bums will be eating in the Ladies' Parlor. The setup is just like it was last night at this time—except there are more people up here.*

His thoughts were interrupted by the approach of Chinese Red, now in the black costume in which he had first seen her. With the black wig, she bore little resemblance to the glamorous person she nightly presented to Chungking Garden patrons.

"Great!" enthused the detective as he surveyed her trim figure, enhanced by the straight-lined clothing of modern Chinese women.

"What are you planning, Mr. Hite?" she asked.

"To catch a rat," he replied succinctly. "Maybe two or three of them. You know where rats hang out the most?"

"I am not wise in the manners of rats," admitted the girl. "Where?"

"In basements," he elucidated. "Come on, Red— we're going down there. The hard way. The way Austen's killer used to take the body downstairs."

Chapter Nineteen

The Hard Way

Chinese Red was silent for a moment. Then she glanced at Quinny with a puzzled expression.

"But you said that Mr. Austen was not killed in Quong Chee's office," she said. "If not—"

"Tony Austen was killed almost where you are standing," replied Quinny, nodding toward the huge urn at her back. "There's where I found the carnation. When he was sick and came out here, he leaned on the brick wall by the crock. The murderer followed him out and stabbed him. Austen fell into the gutter there—last night it had water in it from the rain. One sleeve and the shoulder of his coat were soaking wet from when he fell down, as if he'd fallen on his side."

"But he came back from the terrace into the dining-room and went to the mezzanine—"

"You only think he did," interrupted the detective. "Look, if somebody in a policeman's uniform went past that door there, what would you think? Who, I mean?"

"Why—I'd assume it was a policeman, of course. There's been enough of them around."

"Well, that's the answer. There are a lot more cop uniforms in New York than cops. Lots of people saw Tony Austen go out on the terrace. He had on a white dinner jacket—the only man in Chungking Garden wearing one. Of course, Quong Chee and the waiters had on white coats, but they are all little fellows compared to Austen. Okay. The show goes on. The dining-room is dark. Someone comes from this terrace and goes across the room. He is a tall guy—and he has on a white dinner coat with a red flower in the lapel. *But it wasn't Tony Austen!"*

Chinese Red's lips parted and she looked at the detective in bewilderment.

"Who, then?"

"The man who killed him." Quinny reached up and gave the new derby a tug to bring it down more securely. "That was his first mistake. People always make mistakes in these fancy murders which in the end give the show away. The killer knew Austen was on his way to see Quong Chee in his office. He thought Austen would go across the dining-room to the mezzanine stairs, not knowing Austen always went to the office by way of the checkroom. That was one of the first things that gave me something to think about. Number two— or maybe I thought of it first, at that—was that he was pretty sick with those Nolikker tablets. You don't get over them things in five minutes. It's a cinch no guy who's been having trouble keeping anything on his stomach is going to take any interest in business. This wasn't that urgent.

"Then there was the stuff about the carnation. Peggy Long only thought she saw it when the guy came back from the terrace. What she saw was a spot of blood on the jacket about where the flower had been. The carnation had been knocked off when Austen was stabbed and fell in the gutter, where I found it."

"I don't understand why the murderer should have done all this," protested Chinese Red.

"He had reasons—damn good ones, if things had

gone according to plan, or if he had stuck to it. You see, I figure his original idea was to kill Austen in the office—not on the terrace. He couldn't have known when he was planning this thing that it was going to rain last night so's to keep people off the terrace. The idea was to dope Austen's drink before the victim went up to the office—by the mezzanine stairs, remember. The killer would get up there first by the back way, climb out the window of the inside office, and wait. Pretty soon Austen would join Quong Chee in the other office. About that time Austen would begin to feel lousy—he'd want air. Also privacy. The window would be handy—and the murderer knew the guy didn't want any help when he was feeling that way. There aren't any windows from Quong Chee's office to the roof, only the one in the inner office. Austen would come in there to the window, then the killer would stick him with the knife which he thought was Chinese. There are a lot of people who wouldn't know the difference between a Jap knife and a Chinese one. That includes me. After killing Austen, all he had to do was lam around the roof to the iron steps there and come down to the terrace. No one would know he had been near the office. The Chinese would find the body—and take the rap.

"But things didn't go according to plan, which is generally the case when you figure out a complicated idea to kill somebody. Either he didn't know how quick those pills work, or else Austen crossed him by going out on the terrace. Besides, Quong Chee was waiting for Austen in the foyer instead of the office. The murderer couldn't get to the checkroom stairs on account of this. He had to change his plans quick. By this time Austen had gone to the terrace. He followed him out there and killed him. It was still necessary to his plan to make it look like Austen had gone upstairs. I'll say one thing for this mug, he was a fast thinker—no dumbbell. He put on the white jacket and went up himself, figuring that in the dark while the show was on anyone who saw him would take it for granted that he was Austen. He probably figured that Quong Chee would see him, too, and go to the office. Holding the handkerchief to his mouth was to cover part of his face.

"Up in the office he shed the coat and tucked it away on top of the bookcase. He tossed the knife into the stairway. Then he came back to the terrace over the roof. About this time he commenced to get a new idea. That's one of the weaknesses of people with imagination—before they get done with one plan they think they get a better one. They don't follow through so good. The killer remembered the fake ·opium den downstairs, the bums' clothes on the nail in the little room, and he knew enough about the joint to know Hix's tramps would be eating. Maybe he didn't know this last, but just figured there was a good chance of getting away with what he did. He carried the body downstairs—I'll show you how in a minute—and put it where it was found.

"By this time he had it worked out that if the body was sent off to the morgue as an unidentified Bowery lug, the chances were pretty good that Tony Austen would be just another disappearance case. Anyhow, if the corpse wasn't identified before it was sent away, the clues in Chungking Garden would be cold. All Pierson would have to go on would be that Austen came here on a party, his body was found later in the joint downstairs, and afterward identified in the morgue. What people remember after twenty-four hours have passed ain't reliable—they forget what they saw, and remember things they didn't. It might have been longer than that, too, before the body was identified. About all they would have remembered right would be that the last time they saw him was going upstairs to the office."

"But the coat and knife would have been found sooner or later," the girl pointed out.

"Sure—but by who? Those things wouldn't have been evidence against *him,* even if the cops found 'em. Just insurance for the killer *if* the body was identified before it went to the morgue. See?"

"I don't see what makes you so sure the murder was planned in such detail," said Chinese Red, dubiously. "Couldn't the things you describe have just occurred to him as he went along?"

"That's the hell of it—they could," admitted Quinny. "I'm certain enough that he planned to kill Austen last night, and pretty sure it was done like I just said. I'll know whether I'm wrong in a few minutes, I think."

A couple wandered out to the terrace from the dining-room, sitting at a table at the other end. Quinny glanced at them keenly, but decided it was more likely romance than interest in his affairs that brought them out. He turned to Chinese Red again, taking her by the arm.

"Come on. I'll show you what the killer done after the murder," he said.

They walked to the iron steps at the elevator shaft wall, which formed one of the two walls of the terrace.

Releasing the girl's arm, he ascended the steps. Chinese Red climbed along after him with some difficulty, accepting the helping hand he extended as he reached the roof. In the alley made by the top of the elevator shaft and the steeply slanting roof of the mezzanine, he got out a flashlight, focusing it on the iron-covered door to the shaft. This was closed but not locked, just as he and Pierson had found it the night before. Pulling the door open, Quinny directed the beam of light onto the narrow platform.

"He put the body there," whispered the detective. "And left it while he made the grand tour in Austen's jacket. He went in Quong Chee's office just ahead of me. I thought it was the Chinese. When I went in there wasn't anyone in sight. He had climbed out the window and come back here by way of the roof. Now he takes the clothes off and when the elevator comes up to the restaurant floor he puts the body on top of it. That's where it got streaked up with grease—off the cables. Come on."

Quinny entered the shaft housing, Chinese Red following obediently. Also reluctantly. The elevator was at the restaurant floor and through its grillework top they could see the Chinese boy sitting on a stool at the controls. While they watched, the buzzer sounded and the boy got up to close the doors, preparatory to descent.

Touching his lips with a finger as a sign for the girl not to speak, the detective then took her arm and helped her over to an insecure footing on the top of the elevator at his side. The car started down, Chinese Red clinging fearfully to his arm. As he had hoped, the car continued to the basement without stopping anywhere between. The roof of the elevator was now just a foot or so below the level of the ground floor of the building. The elevator operator underneath them opened his door to admit a couple of passengers.

As silently and quickly as he could manage, Quinny unlatched the ground floor door and peered out. There was no one in the lobby. Then he pulled himself up through the opening and turned to give Chinese Red a hand. He got the door closed again just as the car started to ascend.

"This is as far as he could get the body down with the elevator," said Quinny. "But when he came down the elevator stopped at this floor first."

"How do you know that?" queried the girl.

Quinny started down the stairs to the basement, hidden from the street by the elevator shaft. This stairway wasn't more than a step or two from the elevator door.

"Because I was in it when he came down. I got off at this floor. On the way down I noticed I had a spot of blood on my hand. At first I thought I had scratched it on something, but when I wiped it off there wasn't anything. I didn't think much about it then, but afterward I figured it was a drop of blood that fell through that lattice-work stuff the top of the car is made out of. Moving the body around made it bleed a little again."

He paused on the landing where the basement stairs made a turn.

"You see," he continued, speaking softly, "it wasn't much of a trick to take Austen down to the first floor, then carry him the rest of the way. Nobody saw us now; no one saw him then. He just ducked around the corner of the elevator with the body and was out of sight here in less than a second."

"He must have been strong."

"He was husky enough." Quinny chuckled. "But can you picture me ridin' around with a guy just fresh murdered, and not knowing anything about it?"

Chinese Red shook her head. She was bewildered about what the detective was planning to do and her part in it. Quinny got out a cigarette and some matches, then changed his mind about smoking on the side of caution. While the odor of a cigarette would hardly be noticeable in this incense-filled air, it was just as well not to take any chance of it, he thought. He stuffed the package back into his coat pocket and started down the remaining flight, slowly and carefully. The girl hesitated a moment, then followed.

From the stairs they went to the turn in the hallway. The place was in utter silence, not even any sound issuing from Hix's place, which opened on the gloomy corridor some distance away, beyond the Joss House door. A single incandescent swinging overhead sent flickering shadows over the unpainted walls. In the dark corner where they halted, Chinese Red was hardly visible in her black outfit, only a grayish white spot indicating her face.

"I want you to go in Hix's place and see if there is anyone there you know. In this outfit nobody will recognize you. Don't sneak in—walk right in like you worked there. I'll wait for you in the Joss House. Okay?"

The girl, with a only a slight hesitation, nodded and walked casually down the hall, turning into the doorway beyond the Joss House. Quinny watched her until she had disappeared, then gave his attention to the hall itself. His eyes lighted up as he saw a trail of faintly

glowing spots on the floor between the entrance to the
Joss House and the exit to the yard at the rear of the
building. These had not been visible the night before
when he and Pierson had first explored the basement.
But now only one light burned in the hall. Phosphorescent paint isn't effective where there is much light.

The can of spilled paint in the little room back of
the statue indicated the origin of these spots. Someone
had evidently stepped in it, gone into the hall and up
through the back porches to the restaurant. It seemed
fairly clear to the detective that this must have been the
murderer of Tony Austen. No one else that might have
stepped in the paint would have gone to the restaurant
above. Not the back way.

Quinny walked slowly down the hall, eyeing the
spots, until he reached the Joss House entrance, where
he stopped to look in. The statue of *Chang-o* gleamed
in the semidarkness—the same greenish light given off
by the spots the detective had just been looking at. The
spilled paint evidently was used for touching up the
statue from time to time. But the statue wasn't what
caught Quinny's attention now.

His frowning gaze rested on the broad back of a tall
man, standing between the railing and the statue. Lying on the black wood of the dais near his feet was the
long, slender hand of the goddess, *Chang-o*.

Chapter Twenty

In the Joss House

QUINNY HITE seldom carried a gun. He didn't trust
'em. Considerable practice in police shooting-ranges
and some extracurricular studies in Coney Island shoot-
ing-galleries had convinced him that the only weapon
with destructive potentiality in his hands was a sawed-
off shotgun. As he eyed the back of the man before the
statue, though, he decided that there are times when a
gun would be a comforting bit of equipment, even if
his marksmanship was distinctly low-grade.

As he stood in the doorway considering the problem,
a new development occurred. Another tall figure appeared abruptly from around the side of the statue,
and, as it advanced, the greenish light revealed the grim
features of Mayo Browne, a small automatic held firmly in his right hand.

"Put 'em up, Gates!" snapped Browne, hoarsely.

Gates stepped back, half lifting his hands.

"Nix on the gun, Browne!" he exclaimed. "What's
the idea—"

"The idea is that I thought you would be along after
the money you took from Tony. You damned, dirty,
sneaking—"

"The money *I* took! You're crazy!"

"A little. Crazy to even things up for Tony."

Browne, his eyes narrowed with cold determination,
took a step closer to the terrified newspaper man, who
backed away, twisting his head around as if in search

of help and catching sight of Quinny watching the proceedings from the doorway.

"Hite!" exclaimed Gates in a shaky voice. "Quinny—"

Mayo Browne moved his head and flicked a glance toward the detective. His eyebrows lifted in surprise.

"Just in time, Hite," he greeted. "Seems we've had the same idea about this rat—Tony's murderer—"

"Yeah, I know," responded Quinny, scowling at Gates and coming over from the doorway to stand near Browne. "I was pretty sure of it, too. I was also betting he would come down here to pick up the dough the first chance he got. That's tonight."

Browne nodded shortly. "He killed Tony and hid the money in the statue."

Gates glanced from one to the other of his accusers, licking his lips and breathing heavily.

"No," disagreed Quinny. "That wasn't the way it was—not exactly. The mazuma bracelet was hid in the dragon's mouth, but not by Gates. Dee Forbes saw the Chinese throw an empty cigarette package or something in there. She thought he was the one who killed Tony Austen, so she has a look at the dragon and comes up with the gold band. On account of some bad luck she's had with Austen, she decides this dough is coming to her. She sneaks down here by the back way looking for some place where she can hide it and get at it later. Then she goes back upstairs and tries to put the empty band back where she found it, but this lug waylays her back of the orchestra stand and chokes her. I bet he was mad when he sees the dough ain't in it!"

"If it wasn't Gates who put the band in the dragon, who—"

"You're lying, Hite!" exclaimed Gates, desperately shaking his head. "I—"

"Then you fixed it up afterward with Dee Forbes to split the ten grand," continued Quinny, ignoring interruptions. "You left her in the chop suey place down near the corner. She's gone—I sent her home a little while ago—"

"Did she say I killed Tony Austen?" demanded the newspaper man. "If she did—"

"She didn't accuse anybody, or tell anything," said Quinny. "Hell, I knew what she was waiting there for. I told *her!*"

"We did plan to get the money," admitted Gates, sullenly. "But I don't know anything about the murder. I saw Dee Forbes get the gold band from the dragon, and later I did make a deal with her for a cut. Yes—I know that isn't just according to my Sunday school teaching, but, what the hell—the money wouldn't do Austen any good now—"

"That clears up one point I'd been wondering about," interrupted Browne. "But it doesn't alter the fact that you killed Tony."

"That is a damned lie!" shouted Gates.

"I know exactly how you did this killing," asserted Quinny, staring coldly at the worried columnist. "You doped Austen's drink while he was at your table to make him sick. Then, when he went out on the terrace, you followed him and gave him the knife. You took off his white coat, went across the dining-room and up to the office, threw the knife in the checkroom stairway, put the coat on a shelf, then came back over the roof to the terrace. You were fixing things up for Quong Chee to take the rap. How about it, Browne—that what you figured?"

"Just about," answered Browne. "I didn't work it out in detail. Mine was more of a hunch that this fellow was the murderer. I saw Tony stagger out to the terrace, and I saw this man follow him—"

"Another lie!" Gates broke in. "I was not on that terrace at any time last night!"

"What do you think, Hite?" asked Browne cynically. His eyes remained directed at Gates, the automatic in his hand unwavering.

Quinny shrugged. "I'm all done thinking," he said. "We don't have to try the case here. The thing to do now is send for Inspector Pierson."

"Right!" agreed Mayo Browne.

"Well, you keep this guy covered while I hop over to Hix's joint and telephone. You be careful, too—don't let him make a getaway."

"You needn't worry about that," replied Browne coldly. "Nothing would give me greater pleasure than to pull this trigger."

"For God's sake—" implored Gates.

"Don't do it, unless you have to," cautioned Quinny. "That would put us both in a jam. He's got to stand trial."

"Yes, I know, but he'd better make no attempt to escape."

Quinny strode out of the Joss House, with a backward glance over his shoulder which expressed little confidence that Mayo Browne's fury would not get the better of him. Chinese Red was in the hall. She had completed her mission in the fake opium dive and, returning to report, had heard voices and stopped to listen. Quinny motioned her to follow him. At the door to Hix's part of the basement he stopped and turned to the girl.

"You heard?" he whispered. She nodded. "Go in that closet over there and call Spring 7-3100. Get Inspector Pierson and tell him to lam over here as quick as he can. Okay?"

"Yes." Chinese Red faded silently into the "smoking lounge," and the detective watched her until she disappeared in the telephone closet. Then he walked back to the Joss House entrance.

Browne was standing as he had left him, facing Gates, the latter with his hands still lifted and his eyelids batting with fear. Presently the detective heard the faint noise as Chinese Red left the telephone closet, and he peered through the dusky hallway until her figure appeared. Signaling her to remain where she was, he strode back into the Joss House.

"Okay," he announced. "Pierson's on his way."

"And then this cutthroat's on his way to the chair," gloated Browne. "I hope to be present when they throw the switch!"

"Maybe that can be fixed," said Quinny, with an odd expression in his hazel eyes. "Better give me the gun, Browne—you're nervous and I'm more used to that kind of hardware."

"I'll keep it," replied Browne, tersely. "I was never less nervous in my life. Use your own, if you think I can't handle this one."

"I don't have one," answered Quinny. "Anyhow, one gun's enough in a spot like this—if you're sure you won't get restless with the trigger. Got a cigarette, Browne?"

"There's a package in my right-hand coat pocket.

Help yourself."

Quinny sauntered around behind Browne and thrust his hand into the designated pocket. His lips spread abruptly in a tight grin, and as he brought his hand out with the cigarettes, he dropped the package. His hand darted up between Browne's body and arm, grasping the barrel of the automatic and thrusting it ceilingward. The cartridge exploded noisily and the bullet made a neat, round hole in the plaster overhead. Meanwhile the detective's other arm coiled around Browne's neck.

Long experience had taught Quinny what to expect next. Browne started to bend forward in an effort to toss the detective over his back to the floor. Quinny forestalled this with a sudden lurch against Browne's rear, sending the latter crashing down on his face, with the detective still on his back. A powerful twist removed the weapon from Browne's grasp and the chill steel of the muzzle applied to the prostrate man's neck negated any desire on his part for further struggle.

"What the hell is the idea of this?" shouted Browne.

"I coulda waited for Pierson," Quinny said, from his seat astride Browne. "But I was afraid you'd start think-ing. I made a bad crack a while ago when I said Gates wasn't the one who put the bracelet in the dragon."

Gates, whose knees seemed no longer up to the task of supporting him, had taken a seat on the edge of the black platform, where he sat mopping his forehead with a handkerchief and eyeing the prostrate Browne with a mixture of curiosity and loathing.

"I didn't kill Austen—" mumbled the columnist.

"I know." Quinny got up cautiously from Browne's back, retiring far enough to control the situation with the gun which he hoped devoutly he wouldn't have to shoot. "But, you see, I was afraid Browne here would get wise to the spiel I pulled about you, afraid he'd catch the idea that it was him I was talking about. He's the killer! Outside of tryin' to make off with the cush, you didn't have anything to do with it."

"Wait until Inspector Pierson arrives!" snapped Browne, getting up from the floor. "He'll know what to believe."

"Sure he will," replied the detective. "He's a smart guy. Don't think he ain't."

"He's certainly clever enough to know that I could have nothing to do with this."

"Yeah? Look, dope—when I got it figured out *how* this job was pulled off, it had to be either you or Gates. You two were the only ones connected with Austen who were pretty much the same build—the only ones who could have got away with wearing his coat across the dining-room and making people who knew Austen believe it was him. Also, you were the only outsiders that knew enough about Chungking Garden to stage this murder the way it was done."

"But why me?" demanded Browne. "Granting what you say, why not Gates? He had incentive—he tried to kill Austen at the Bantam Bar night before last. Or do you remember? Gates also knew that Tony had a lot of money on him."

"Sure, Gates tried to brain Austen with a bottle," admitted Quinny, imperturbably. "But even if he had got away with it, that wouldn't have been murder. Manslaughter, maybe. A man does things in a fight that he wouldn't do any other time. You had plenty of reasons to kill Austen. The kind of reasons that kept on getting

bigger the more you thought about 'em. He was in
your way. If it hadn't been for him cutting in, you
might have grabbed off Fane Gordon and her dough
for yourself. You needed dough to put the Camonez
romance over. The ten grand would of done it, probably. Austen held some bad checks of yours and was
cashing in on them by making you his stooge for anything he didn't want to do himself. You hated his guts.
Gates maybe didn't like Austen much, but that ain't
murder motive.

"I've got more than that, too. You came down here
last night on this party without a watch. I've got a wit-
ness for that. But after the murder, you did have a
watch—and that watch was Austen's. I got a description of it this afternoon. Why you were dopey enough
to wear it, I don't know—except maybe you figured
that nobody pays much attention to a wrist watch on a
man's arm. The only reason I did was because I knew
you came downtown without one. Later you planted
it on Dave Kelton.

"Then there was that business about the knife. You
pulled another dumb one trying to be smart. That
knife came out of the showcase at Mrs. Barwin's. It's a
hara-kiri knife—Jap, not Chinese, like you thought it
was. You were thinking of pinning the murder on
Quong Chee when you stole the knife. Gates couldn't
have snitched the knife, since he wouldn't have been in
Mrs. Barwin's house since she gave up having parties—
if he ever had been there. Mrs. Barwin told me this,
and she said you've been there plenty.

"When we take a look at your dress shoes, we're going to find some of this green paint on 'em, picked up
in the back room there where you took Austen's body

to switch his clothes. If we're lucky, we're also going to find the shirt you wore, which most likely got some blood on it from Austen's coat when you put it on after killing him.

"Most murderers are dopes—no matter how smart they are any other time. They kill somebody because they ain't smart enough to figure out any other way to get what they want." Quinny paused to listen to a sound in the hall. "That'll be Inspector Pierson."

Browne's face was a picture of indecision for a second as the scuffle of sturdy feet approached the entrance to the Joss House. Then with reckless and foolhardy courage, he threw himself at the detective. Quinny, however, was not taken by surprise. He simply avoided Browne's headlong rush, and the man, losing his balance, stumbled to his knees, then went into a full-length sprawl, face downward at Pierson's feet as the inspector came into the room.

"What in—" Pierson started to exclaim, but the instinct begotten of years of police work took charge. He reached down and found a strangling hold on Browne's collar, jerking him into a sitting position. "What is this?"

"You got a fistful of murderer," replied Quinny. "That is the mug which knocked off Austen. He said a while ago he wanted us to fix it for him to be on hand in the death house when the switch was thrown. I'm accommodating. He'll be there."

Pierson's gray eyes scrutinized Quinny closely as he turned his prisoner over to one of his aids. "You're sure?"

"Sure, I'm sure." Quinny handed the gun to one of Pierson's plain-clothes men. "Here, take this. I don't like the damn things—shot myself in the hip pocket with one once."

"How about this fellow here?" Pierson glowered at the hapless Gates. "Is he mixed up in it?"

"He's mixed up in it—but he didn't have anything to do with the murder," said Quinny. "You can skip him. Browne was just fixing to kill him when I showed up."

"Why?"

"Well, I don't think that was what was on his mind when he came down here tonight. I figure he came for the dough, but he didn't know where it was after Dee Forbes snitched it out of the dragon. He just had an idea it was in this room somewhere, so he hid himself back of the statue in the hope she'd show up for it. He can change plans quick. When he saw Gates he made a new one, deciding to make Gates the fall guy for the murder, on account of he'd heard Quong Chee was released."

A stifled exclamation escaped Gates's tight lips.

"You didn't know that, Gates," Quinny went on. "This mug was going to knock you off and give out the news that he had discovered the murderer. There wouldn't have been much you could have done about it—he'd have made a good case."

"See here, Quinny," exclaimed Pierson. "Suppose you go back to the beginning and give me the whole works, instead of these bits and pieces."

Quinny gave him the works.

QUINNY FINISHED making his case against Mayo Browne and Inspector Pierson, amply satisfied, took over. Men were dispatched to search Browne's room uptown, later to report to their chief with the phosphorus-stained dress shoes and the blood-marked shirt, as well as two empty Nolikker capsules found in Browne's dinner jacket. Apparently the man had never realized he might be suspected of complicity in the murder of his friend.

Chinese Red was in the hallway as Quinny came out. She had been listening.

"All over," greeted Quinny, taking her arm and giving it a friendly squeeze. "We can go up and tell Quong Chee he ain't got anything to worry about now. Not even his lease."

"He will be relieved," said the girl.

Quinny thought her answer smacked of understatement, but on the other hand, these Chinese didn't seem to get very excited about things. Maybe that was it.

"I was not able to report to you what I saw in Mr. Hix's place," she said, as though it could still be of importance.

"What did you see?"

"I found that all the tramps were in the Ladies' Parlor having dinner. Two of them I should like for you to see."

Quinny stared at her curiously. What on earth could

any of these phony dopesters have to do with the murder now, he wondered. Without asking, he walked into the "smoking lounge" and to the Ladies' Parlor beyond, with Chinese Red trotting along right behind him. She was laughing, although Quinny didn't know it. He jerked open the door of the parlor and looked in, his gaze roaming over the scattered assembly of waifs.

Two of these held his attention. They were dressed in clothes obviously made disreputable for purposes of masquerade. The food piled on their plates was receiving exceedingly indifferent attention, and as they saw Quinny standing in the doorway they lost interest in eating entirely. The detective grinned affably at the brothers Kelton.

"Hiya, boys!" he greeted. "See you finally got some work you can do. Congratulations. But if you was figuring on any other kind of work down here, skip it and go home. The party is over."

There were fewer people in the dining-room of Chungking Garden when Chinese Red and Quinny returned. The floor show had begun and finished while they were downstairs, and a large number of the diners had gone on to other amusement.

"Why," began Chinese Red as they reached the mezzanine on the way to Quong Chee's apartment, "did you take me on this strange journey? Did you know you were going to find those men there?"

"I expected to find 'em—one of 'em, anyway. But not so soon as we did. I thought both of them would show up on account of, though Mayo Browne was the killer, they were both on the search for the ten grand. That's all that got either of 'em down here tonight. Even those dumb Kelton boys were having a go at it. I admit the stakes was good! What I wanted you for, besides having a yen for your company, was to have somebody that could give Hix's joint the once over without being recognized, because I thought that would be the way they'd try to get to the Joss House. You know, come down on a bus just like any other sightseer."

He paused, his hand on the apartment doorknob. "I didn't figure on getting into the spot I did, though. I had to do a lot of fast thinking when Browne came up with the gun. I had to make him think I believed it was Gates who killed Austen, and be careful not to overdo it, too. But you know all about that—now."

"You were very convincing," returned the girl. "You made me think it was Sherry Gates."

The detective grinned. "I guess that makes you the first dame I ever fooled, then," he said, twisting the knob and opening the door. "I oughta save you. You know, it's a lot easier to fool a guy than it is a woman, on account of a man listens to what you say. So does a woman, but she makes her decisions on something else—"

"Intuition?"

"I guess. I'd just call it a hunch."

Quong Chee was still in the small library where they had left him, poring over a huge book the pages of which were filled with exquisitely executed Chinese characters. He looked up as they entered. Quinny rendered an account of the events of the past half hour. The Chinese, inexpressibly relieved that he was no longer an object of interest to police, exchanged the large tome for a much smaller book in which the words were printed in English. In short, a checkbook, the nucleus of any good library.

At the elevator as the detective took leave of the Chinese and his lovely ward, Quong Chee shook hands gravely.

"It is my hope that you will visit us again," he said. "And under less disturbing conditions."

Quinny glanced at the girl. She extended her hand, and the detective discovered that it felt nice in his. Exceptionally nice. You didn't have to be a detective to realize that.

"How about you, babe?" he asked.

"Me cwy lu, too," she said.

The irrepressible Honey Joe was on the sidewalk when the detective came down. A large busload of people had just filed down to view the dreadful spectacle of the opium den, and having made sure that they were all thus headed in the right direction and not wandering off on their own to competitive enterprises, Hix was about to follow. He caught sight of the detective and halted on the top step to the basement.

"Hey, Quinny!" he called, and the detective veered over in his direction. "I hear it's all over—that you landed the murderer."

"Of course," admitted Quinny. "What did you think —that I was going to let him get away with it?"

"Boy, what a stunt for my business!" enthused the ex-pitchman. "What a honey! Tomorrow I'm gonna put in a wax dummy to play Tony Austen in the murder bunk—and will the yokels flood the joint! Wow!"

Quinny grinned. "Why don't you cut the overhead and put in a lot of wax dummies instead of the flophouse bums?"

"Say, that's a honey of an idea, at that." Hix screwed up his forehead. "A honey. Bums are gettin' scarce—first-class bums, anyway. The ones I'm gettin' lately are a disgrace to the place. Say, lug, you know what I'm gonna do for you for fixin' everything up all neat and tidy like this? I ain't the kind of guy which forgets what his friends done for him. Not Honey Joe—no, sir! Here, take these."

He thrust a couple of pieces of soiled cardboard into Quinny's hand.

"What is it?" asked the detective, peering at the gift.

"Free passes on the Chinatown bus—come down any time, brother—and bring a friend—to see the horrors of a Chinatown opium den. All new next week beginnin' with— Well, anyway, come down—it's on the house."

"Thanks, Joe," returned Quinny. "Maybe I will. But not to see horrors. I get enough of them. I could do with another look at the Chinese girl with red hair, though." He paused to grin at Hix. "Now, there's a *real* honey!"

The lovely charm of Chinese Red, though, wasn't on Quinny's mind as he subwayed back to his familiar Thirty-ninth Street. A more urgent problem pricked at his otherwise satisfied feeling.

What, he pondered, *does a guy have to do to keep the dame he's in love with from lamming off to San Francisco on him? And this love stuff, does a mug get all right after a while—or does it get worse? I'll have to hunt up Johnny Littlebird—women and love is all he knows anything about, and I guess I don't know very much about either. Murder is my dish.*